JOE COLTON'S JOURNAL

I am enormously grateful that my niece, Heather McGrath, has come to Hacienda de Alegria, for a short sabbatical. With so many troubles befalling the family, I need all the emotional support I can get right now. Once I thought the Colton empire was indestructible, but now that another attempt has been made on my life, I wonder how much longer I'll be around to keep the Colton clan together. Fortunately, the investigating detective, Thaddeus Law, has sworn to see justice done and to keep us all safe. He seems to be particularly interested in keeping an eye on Heather, even though he does an awful good impression of the big bad wolf whenever she's around. My sheltered niece is hardly this world-weary single dad's type, but unless my sight is starting to fail, I swear I see stars glistening in her blue eyes whenever Thad storms into a room. Could my sweet and innocent niece have finally found her Prince Charming in the form of this dark and brooding lawman?

About the Author

RUTH LANGAN

is an award-winning, bestselling author of more than sixty books, both contemporary and historical and has been described by *Romantic Times Magazine* as "a true master at involving your emotions, be they laughter or tears." Four of Ruth's books have been finalists for the Romance Writers of America's RITA Award. Over the years, she has given dozens of print, radio and TV interviews, including some for *Good Morning America* and *CNN News*, and has been quoted in such diverse publications as the *Wall Street Journal*, *Cosmopolitan* and the *Detroit Free Press*. Married to her childhood sweetheart, she has raised five children and lives in Michigan, the state where she was born and raised. She hopes her readers will love her warm and wonderful characters in *Passion's Law* as much as she does.

Passion's
Law

Ruth
Langan

Silhouette Books

Published by Silhouette Books
America's Publisher of Contemporary Romance

Special thanks and acknowledgment are given
to Ruth Langan for her contribution
to THE COLTONS series.

SILHOUETTE BOOKS
300 East 42nd St.,
New York, N. Y. 10017

ISBN 0-373-38709-1

PASSION'S LAW

Visit Silhouette at www.eHarlequin.com

Printed in U.S.A.

THE
COLTONS

Meet the Coltons—
a California dynasty with a legacy of privilege and power.

Heather McGrath: *A country club dilettante.* Though she's lived a charmed life, Joe Colton's foster niece's two broken engagements have made her despair of ever meeting her Prince Charming. Until she runs into a hunky single dad who seems to be just what Cupid ordered!

Thaddeus Law: *A jaded detective.* A far cry from the smooth-faced, golden boys Heather has been dating in San Diego, and a decade older, this lawman just might be her diamond in the rough.

Silas "Snake Eyes" Pike: *A conniving little weasel.* Hired by Meredith Colton's evil twin sister to find Emily Blair, this hit man has just tracked her down to Keyhole, Wyoming....

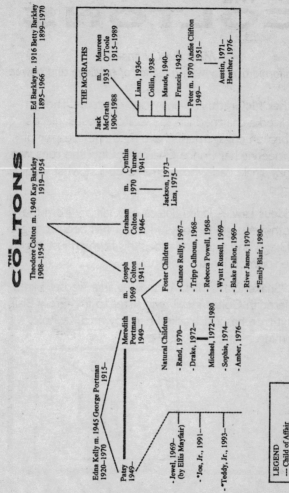

THE COLTONS

Theodore Colton m. 1940 Kay Barkley — Ed Barkley m. 1916 Betty Barkley
1908–1954   1919–1954   1895–1966   1899–1970

Edna Kelly m. 1945 George Portman   Joseph Colton m. 1969 Graham Colton m. 1970 Cynthia Turner
1920–1970   1915–   1941–   1946–   1941–

Meredith Portman 1949–

Patsy 1949–

Foster Children
- Chance Reilly, 1967–
- Tripp Calhoun, 1968–
- Rebecca Powell, 1968–
- Wyatt Russell, 1969–
- Blake Fallon, 1969–
- River James, 1970–
- *Emily Blair, 1980–

Natural Children
- Rand, 1970–
- Drake, 1972–
- Michael, 1972–1980
- Sophie, 1974–
- Amber, 1976–

- Jewel, 1969– (by Ellis Mayfair)
- *Joe, Jr., 1991–
- *Teddy, Jr., 1993–

Jackson, 1973–
Liza, 1975–

THE McGRATHS

Jack McGrath m. Maureen O'Toole
1906–1988   1935   1915–1989

Liam, 1936–
Collin, 1938–
Maude, 1940–
Francis, 1942–
Peter m. 1970 Andie Clifton
1949–   1951–

Austin, 1971–
Heather, 1976–

LEGEND
--- Child of Affair
━ Twins
• Adopted by Joe Colton

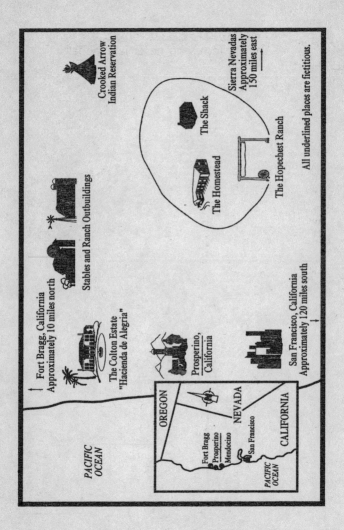

PACIFIC
OCEAN

Fort Bragg, California
Approximately 10 miles north

Stables and Ranch Outbuildings

The Colton Estate
"Hacienda de Alegria"

Prosperino,
California

San Francisco, California
Approximately 120 miles south

Crooked Arrow
Indian Reservation

The Shack

The Homestead

Sierra Nevadas
Approximately
150 miles east

The Hopechest Ranch

All underlined places are fictitious.

OREGON

NEVADA

CALIFORNIA

Fort Bragg
Prosperino
Mendocino
San Francisco

PACIFIC
OCEAN

For Nora, who keeps challenging me to fly.
And for Tom, who never lets me fall.

One

"Hey. Where did you go just now?" Peter Mc-Grath, Chief Financial Officer of Colton Enterprises, easily maneuvered the car around a curve in the road and glanced over at his daughter, Heather, who was staring pensively out the window. "What are you thinking, honey?"

Heather watched the passing scenery with keen interest. "Just thinking how big California is. And how different it looks once we leave San Diego."

"I hope you're not regretting your decision to come here and give your Uncle Joe a hand with his business affairs."

She gave her father a gentle smile. "Of course not. In fact, I was thinking just the opposite. There's such rugged beauty here. I'm glad I'll have some time to really see it. You know I've always loved the ranch. As for Uncle Joe, I'm happy to help. Really."

Peter was delighted by his daughter's response. He had a special love for his foster brother, Joe Colton. Joe had been the one to see to Peter's education at one of the best universities in the country, and been enormously proud of Peter's intelligence, especially his mathematical talents. After graduation from Stanford, Peter happily accepted a low-level job in the accounting department of Colton Shipping. Because he proved to be a whiz at finding loopholes and shelters in the corporate tax laws, he quickly came to the attention of his supervisors, who sang his praises to Joe. Joe in turn gave Peter free rein within the company, and Peter had soon worked his way up the corporate ranks of Colton Enterprises. This put Peter in a position to repay his foster brother many times over by acting as a diligent watchdog on Joe Colton's behalf.

There was a special bond between these two men. One that had always grated on Joe Colton's blood brother, Graham.

Peter reached over to lay a hand on Heather's. "That's my girl."

He turned the car up the familiar long, winding driveway and came to a stop in front of the large, sand-colored adobe house. "Welcome to Hacienda de Alegria."

Heather smiled, showing her dimples. "House of Joy."

Her father's smile faded slightly. "There hasn't been much of that here lately." He sighed before switching off the ignition and shoving open the car door.

Heather knew he was thinking about the summer birthday party for her uncle, and the shocking attempt on Joe Colton's life. She tucked her arm through her father's as they started up the walk together. "Then maybe we can change that."

They were met at the front door by Meredith Colton, Joe's wife. Her brown eyes seemed to narrow at the sight of them. "What are you doing here?"

"Meredith." Peter stepped closer, to kiss her cheek, but she stepped back, avoiding him. "Joe's expecting us."

She nodded. "Business, I suppose."

"That's part of it. But mostly we're here because we're family, and Joe needs us."

She turned away without even acknowledging Peter's words and completely ignored his daughter. "Joe's in his office, I expect. That's where he seems to spend all his time these days."

She walked away, leaving them staring after her. The housekeeper, Inez, beckoned, leading them through the central courtyard where a fountain splashed and flowers grew in profusion in dozens of containers.

"Now that was a warm welcome," Heather whispered.

"Nothing we didn't expect. She and Joe were probably fighting again. They seem to do a lot of that lately. It's obvious the tension is getting to both of them."

Peter kept his arm around his daughter's shoulders as they walked along a cool, dim hallway and paused before ornately carved double doors. The housekeeper knocked once, then opened the doors and stood aside, allowing them to enter.

"Joe." Peter's smile was back, brighter than ever. Joe Colton may not be blood-related, but he meant the world to the younger man, who had always looked up to him.

Across the room Joe Colton, seated behind a massive desk, shoved back his chair and sprang to his feet to hurry across the room.

"Peter. I've been watching for you." Joe caught the younger man in a great bear hug, before holding him a little away to look him over. "You're looking good."

"Thanks. So are you."

Joe turned to Heather and embraced her warmly. "Hello, sweetheart. It was generous of you to offer your help."

She gave him a hard, quick hug before looking up into his smiling eyes. "I'm happy to do it, Uncle Joe."

The older man kept hold of his niece's hand as he led her toward his desk. It was then that Heather realized they weren't alone.

A man got to his feet beside one of the high-backed leather chairs, watching with a quiet intensity that Heather found disconcerting.

"Thad Law, this is my little brother Peter McGrath." Joe saw the man's brow arch and was quick to add, "We have different last names because we're not blood brothers. But the bond is the same, wouldn't you say, Pete?"

"You bet. Even stronger than blood." Peter gave a firm nod of his head.

Joe added, "Pete, this is Police Detective Thaddeus Law."

As the two men shook hands it was Peter's turn to arch a brow. "Police detective? Has there been more trouble?"

Joe patted his brother's arm. "Now don't go making a big deal of this. We just had some things to discuss." He drew Heather closer. "Thad, this is

Peter's daughter, Heather. She's agreed to live here for a while and act as my assistant.''

''Miss McGrath.'' There was that intense look again. As though he were dissecting her, inch by inch.

Heather forced a smile as she offered her hand. ''Detective Law.''

His big hand engulfed hers and she felt a quick rush of heat that left her startled. When she looked up to see if he'd felt it as well, he abruptly shifted his gaze to her uncle.

She used the opportunity to study his profile. A wide forehead. Strong, chiseled features. A jaw that jutted with an air of determination. Jet black hair cut military-short.

He wasn't handsome in the classic sense, but he was an imposing figure, not just because of his size, but because of some unfathomable air of command. It was obvious to anyone looking at him that even without a uniform he was a cop.

His voice was deep, the words spoken in a staccato delivery, as though by someone accustomed to giving orders rather than taking them. ''I'll go over the information you gave me, and get back to you tomorrow, Senator.''

Joe's smile was quick. ''I told you, Thad. That part of my life is long over. It's just plain Joe now.''

The detective nodded. ''Okay, Joe. I'll talk to you

tomorrow. On my way out, I'll look over your security system, and see if I can find any flaws."

The two men shook hands. As the detective stepped away, he turned the full force of that steady gaze on Heather once again, and she felt the heat rise to her cheeks. But only because, she told herself firmly, she'd been caught staring.

Peter waited until they were alone before asking, "What's going on, Joe?"

The older man shrugged. "Nothing to worry about. Thad was one of the first detectives on the scene when that shot was fired at my party. He's been back ever since, combing for clues they might have missed. Obviously he's not happy with some of the things he's found. I like the way he works. I had a few things I wanted him to check for me."

Peter's voice lowered. "You worried about something, Joe?"

"What? Me worry?" Joe gave an easy laugh. "Come on, Pete. Let's have a drink and then we'll enjoy some lunch in the courtyard." He opened a cabinet and pulled out a crystal decanter. "Heather, will you join us?"

His niece shook her head. "No thanks. I think I'll walk around and get reacquainted with your beautiful home, Uncle Joe. I'll be back in time to join the two of you for lunch."

She let herself out of the office and strolled to the

courtyard, pausing to watch the play of sunlight on the fountain. It was such a pretty picture, with the pots of colorful flowers and trailing ivy. The cool tile, the expanse of glass, the sound of water all added to a feeling of peace and serenity.

She strolled through the great room and paused at the windows, crossing her arms over her chest as she studied the magnificent view in the distance. The lush valley. Rolling green hills. Oh, it was so pleasant here. So perfect.

It was hard to believe that in this serene setting there was so much seething hostility. So much pain. Her uncle had lost a son to death, an adopted daughter to a kidnapping. And then there was the horrible attempt that had been made on his life. As yet, no one had been arrested. But Uncle Joe had, as always, tried to take the high road, downplaying the incident, insisting that they'd all made too much of it.

She didn't believe him, of course. Being the target of an assassin's bullet would leave a person traumatized. But it was obvious that Joe Colton was determined to get on with his life, and to locate his daughter, Emily.

That factor had weighed heavily in Heather's decision to move here. She knew how much her father loved Joe Colton, and how concerned he was. She shared that love and concern. If her presence here could ease his burden even a little, then she would stay here for as long as he needed her.

As for her Aunt Meredith's cool reception, she'd already decided not to let that bother her. Her aunt had changed in the past few years. Everyone had noticed it. Meredith had become caught up in herself and her own selfish needs. Heather would simply keep her distance from her aunt and concentrate on what her uncle needed.

She already knew the business. After college she'd gone to work for her father, in the financial department of Colton Enterprises. She'd proven herself efficient, good with figures, and a quick study. There wasn't anything she couldn't do if she set her mind to it.

She sighed, thinking about the life she'd left behind. It had been so easy to adapt to her family's charmed lifestyle. She knew her mother had several young men already picked out as potential husbands for her. Her friends thought it so amusing, especially since she'd been engaged twice and had both times broken the engagement after only weeks. She never let those around her see the pain and confusion she'd suffered. How could they understand? Heather had dreams of her own. Dreams she hadn't shared with anyone, even her adored brother, Austin.

Austin. How she ached for him. She was probably the only one who could see that behind that angry, brooding facade, he was hiding a broken heart. She would give anything to help him. But she knew, with a woman's instincts, that he would have to find his own way through the maze that his life had become.

She was suddenly relieved that she'd agreed to come here. Not only could she help her favorite uncle, but this might also prove to be the perfect break from a lifestyle that had become almost too hectic, too crammed with parties and lunches and activities. And complications, she thought grimly. A mother determined to get her only daughter married to the right man, someone who would fit in with their upscale lifestyle. And a father who adored his only daughter and was far too willing to pull strings to get her whatever her heart desired.

The problem was, she wasn't certain just what she wanted. She knew only what she didn't want. She didn't want the empty life her friends were living, and though she adored her parents, she wanted more than the life her mother lived.

Unlike her Aunt Meredith, who had allowed herself to become caught up in the pursuit of happiness to the exclusion of those around her, Heather yearned for something else. Something simpler. Right now, living and working here at her uncle's ranch, without having to deal with outside influences, could be the antidote she'd been seeking.

Heather wasn't sure how long she'd been standing there, lost in thought, when she sensed that she wasn't alone. She whirled and found herself face to face with a scowling Thad Law.

"Detective." She brought a hand to her throat in a gesture of surprise. "I didn't hear you."

There was a breathy quality to her voice that intrigued him. If he hadn't noticed it earlier in her uncle's office, he'd write it off as nerves. Without realizing it, his frown deepened. He took a step closer, until they were mere inches apart.

With each step that he took toward her, she had an almost overpowering urge to step back, out of reach. Foolish, she knew, but the feeling was too strong to deny. This man made her uncomfortable. Odd, since she'd never before been anything but completely comfortable in the presence of men. But then, this man wasn't like any she'd ever met.

Though she thought of herself as tall, she had to tip her head back to see his face. He had to be several inches over six feet, with broad shoulders and a powerfully muscled chest. For a big man he moved with surprising catlike grace.

"Sorry. I didn't mean to startle you." His voice was low and deep, with a hint of impatience.

"You could have warned me you were here." She had the distinct impression that he'd been there for some time, watching her, and had been as uncomfortable as she when she'd turned and caught sight of him.

"And interrupt those deep thoughts of yours?"

So, he had been watching her.

When he drew close she saw again that piercing stare. It had the strangest effect on her. She'd thought his eyes dark, but in the sunlight streaming through the windows she could see that they were a deep midnight blue.

A breeze flitted through the open window, flinging a lock of her hair across her face. Without warning he lifted a finger to it and brushed it aside. It was the slightest touch, and yet it sent a jolt of electricity charging through her system with all the force of a lightning bolt.

At that simple touch she stood perfectly still, absorbing the tremors that rocked her. Her eyes widened and she had to clasp her hands together to keep from flinching.

Had he felt it, too, or was she the only one affected like this? A quick glance at his face revealed only a slight narrowing of his eyes. But it was enough to tell her that he wasn't as cool and disinterested as he tried to appear.

He cleared his throat. "Did I understand that you're going to be living here?"

She nodded, afraid to trust her voice.

"For how long?"

She swallowed and prayed she wouldn't sound as uneasy as she felt. "I don't really know." She looked at him, then away. "I guess I'll be here for as long as my uncle needs me."

"Needs you for what?"

"He's been spending most of his time here since the..." She couldn't bring herself to mention the shooting. "Since his party. And because I'm familiar with the work, I offered to come here and act as his assistant."

"I see." He glanced around. "Have you considered the isolation of this place?"

She nodded. "That's part of its charm."

"For a week or two maybe. After that, when people realize they can't shop at high-priced boutiques, or reserve a table at a fancy restaurant, the charm starts to wear thin. How long do you think you can stand it, Miss McGrath?"

"I told you. For as long as my uncle needs me."

"Even if it turns out to be months?"

She nodded. "That's right." She arched a brow. "Is that a look of skepticism, Detective?"

"Could be. Personally I doubt you'll last more than a week or two before you get the urge to race back to civilization."

"Is that so? You wouldn't care to bet on that, would you?"

For the first time his lips curved slightly, the only

hint of humor. "Are you asking a man of the law to gamble?"

"Afraid you'll lose?"

He continued staring at her. "Are you a betting woman, Miss McGrath?"

"I've been known to make a wager or two."

"Have you now?" He gave her a measuring look that had the heat rising to her cheeks. "Five bucks says you're bored out of your mind and out of here within two weeks." He stuck out his hand. "Deal?"

She glanced down at his hand, then up into those challenging eyes. "Oh, yeah. How can I resist such an easy way to make five dollars? You're on, Detective."

He closed his hand over hers and, too late, she remembered how she'd felt the first time his hand had held hers. The heat was back, racing along her spine, surging through her veins. But when she tried to pull free, he merely drew her closer, until his lips hovered just above hers. "My friends call me Thad."

"Really?" She wanted to look away, but wouldn't give him the satisfaction. Instead she lifted her head, forcing herself to meet that steely gaze. "Then I guess I'll call you Detective Law, because I don't see the two of us becoming friends. Would you like to pay up now? Or are you going to make me wait until the two weeks are up?"

He chuckled. He'd give her this much. She didn't back down. "You haven't won anything yet, Miss McGrath. As for me, I think my job just got more interesting."

"Your job?" She was suddenly alert as she yanked her hand free and studied him more carefully. "You're...working here? I thought this was just a routine visit, and that you wouldn't be back."

"Sorry to disappoint you."

For the first time she noticed the notepad in his other hand. Her voice lowered. "If this isn't merely a routine check, does this mean something is wrong?"

He kept his features deliberately unreadable. "Sorry, Miss McGrath. I'm not at liberty to discuss my business with anyone except your uncle."

"Of course." She felt the sting of censure and wondered how it was that this man could make her feel so damnably awkward. In any other man his attitude would come across as pure arrogance, but she had the feeling that in Thad Law, it was simply the way he conducted business. No doubt he put up a wall between himself and every civilian he came in contact with.

"Well." She took a step back, needing to put some distance between them so she could catch her breath. "Don't let me stop you, Detective."

Instead of giving her the space she so obviously

wanted, he leaned close and watched the way her eyes narrowed. "I told you. It's Thad. Why don't you try it?"

"Why don't you—" She drew in a breath when she saw the hint of humor in his eyes. She counted to ten, then tried again. "Okay. Why not? I guess I'll be seeing you around, Thad."

"You can count on it, Miss McGrath."

"My name is Heather."

He seemed to consider that a moment, as though fitting the name to the woman. "You can count on seeing me around, Heather." He stood there a moment longer, feeling the tension hum between them. Then he turned on his heel.

She watched him walk away. It occurred to her that he didn't so much walk as stalk. Like a panther on the trail of some poor, unsuspecting prey.

She shivered at the thought.

Crossing her arms over her chest, she waited until her breathing had returned to normal and her legs felt steady enough to carry her without stumbling. Then she headed in the opposite direction. She didn't want to bump into Thaddeus Law again. There was something far too dark and dangerous about him.

Like a man who'd seen too much. And knew too many secrets. Secrets he had no intention of sharing with anyone.

But then, why should he? A man like that probably didn't need anyone or anything. He gave every impression of being a law unto himself.

Thad headed toward Joe's office. But though he mechanically noted the security sensors positioned overhead, his mind was still on Heather McGrath. When she'd first stepped into Joe Colton's office, he'd felt like some sort of awestruck schoolboy. She was almost too perfect. Like every man's ideal woman. Tall, willowy, with soft blue eyes and a turned-up nose. She even had perfect dimples when she smiled. And to top it off, all that smooth blond hair flowing like silk.

He'd had to touch it. Just to assure himself it was as soft as it looked. The jolt he'd been forced to endure had been worth it. It was the kind of hair a man wanted to sink his hands into.

And then there were those lips. So perfectly formed. The lower lip full and inviting. He'd been shocked by the urge to kiss her, to touch his mouth to hers and drink his fill.

The perfume she wore was intoxicating. Like crushed roses. When he'd breathed her in, she went straight to his head and sent it spinning.

A man could get addicted to a woman like that.

He'd been grateful for those few minutes to study

her when she'd first arrived. It had given him the
advantage when they'd been introduced.

Of course, that didn't explain why he'd spent all
that time studying her again when he'd come upon
her just now.

He frowned. Men didn't need a reason to look at
a woman like that. It was the most natural thing in
the world. And it wasn't as if she didn't know she
was beautiful. How could she not be aware of it?
She'd probably been stared at by men since she was
old enough to wiggle those sexy hips.

He knew her type. In his line of work he'd come
across dozens of women like her. Rich, pampered,
adored. They took their beauty and their lifestyle for
granted. And when things started to fall apart, so did
they.

He'd be willing to bet that her idea of work was
leeching off her rich uncle and talking endlessly on
the phone to her friends. The first time she broke a
fingernail she'd probably throw a tantrum.

Still, when they shook hands, he'd felt the heat
clear to his toes. There was no denying she was one
hot little female.

And, he figured, as long as he was going to be
here conducting an investigation, he may as well
enjoy the view. Even though he'd have to remember
not to touch.

Heather McGrath was too rich for his blood.

He knocked, then opened the door when he heard Joe Colton's voice summon him to enter.

"What'd you find, Thad?"

"It's a good security system, as far as it goes. But I'd recommend that you add some refinements."

Joe nodded. "Okay. That's why I asked for your help. How soon can you have it done to your satisfaction?"

Thad shrugged. "A day or two. I can order the parts you need. If you don't mind, I'd like to hire the workmen myself. No sense having strangers on the premises that haven't passed a security check."

Joe smiled. "Whatever you say, Thad. Can you stay for lunch?"

"No, thanks." Thad turned away. "I'll see you first thing in the morning."

When the door closed behind him, Peter McGrath gave Joe a long, measuring look. "Seems to me you're going to a lot of trouble for a man who doesn't think anything's wrong."

Joe clapped a hand on his foster brother's shoulder. "After what's happened lately, I've decided to wise up and take precautions. Besides, my favorite niece plans on living and working here now. I'd like to think that all these security measures will give you and Andie some peace of mind."

Peter nodded, thinking of the way his wife, Andie, had reacted when she'd heard what Heather planned to do. She liked having her daughter close. "You're right, of course. I'm grateful that you're finally ready to put your safety in the hands of an expert."

At the appearance of the housekeeper, Inez, announcing that lunch was ready, the two men made their way to the beautiful dining room, overlooking the courtyard. They met Heather just coming from the other direction.

"Will Aunt Meredith be joining us?" she called cheerfully.

Joe shook his head. "Meredith never eats lunch here. In fact, she's rarely at home. That's just one more reason why I'm so glad you're here, sweetheart. You'll be great company. Besides, your father assures me that you're an expert at whipping an office into shape."

As the three were seated they could see, through the floor-to-ceiling windows, Thaddeus Law walking to his car.

"Speaking of experts." Peter nodded toward the figure of the officer. "I wouldn't want to mess with Detective Law. He looks like he could take on an entire gang of gunmen without flinching."

"Yeah." Joe laughed. "And spit out their bullets if they were foolish enough to fire at him."

The two men shared a laugh while Heather merely watched in silence as the man they were discussing tossed his jacket on the passenger seat before stepping inside and driving away in a cloud of dust.

Somehow she had the impression that her father and uncle weren't too far from the truth.

Two

Heather showered and dressed quickly, in a simple turtleneck and jeans, eager to begin her first day at the ranch. She ran a brush through her hair and tied it back with a clip, then let herself out of her room and danced barefoot down the stairs.

She knew that the tender farewell scene with her father yesterday had been much harder on him than on her. He'd felt that he was losing his baby, and had actually said as much. For her part, she felt only a sense of freedom. For the next few weeks or months she would have no commitments. Her only responsibility was to her uncle and his business affairs. That was a level of comfort that suited her far more than the corporate setting she'd had to adapt to for the past couple of years.

She smiled to herself. She was sick of business suits and cramming her feet into high-heeled pumps. Bored with long-winded presentations and working lunches. Weary of dressing up at night for black-tie charity events, and making small talk with high-powered executives who always seemed to have one eye on the media.

In the kitchen she was thrilled to discover that she was the first one up. She plugged in the coffeemaker before rummaging through the cupboards. When she located some cereal she poured a bowl, topped it with milk, and grabbed up a spoon before heading out the door. On the porch she settled herself on the top step and leaned her back against the railing, enjoying the spectacular sunrise while she ate.

The sky was ablaze with ribbons of pink and mauve and deep purple. The air was warm and dry, with just a hint of the perfume of jewel-colored dianthus and ivy in nearby terracotta planters.

Heather saw a blur of movement out of the corner of her eye and turned to look, her spoon halfway to her mouth. She nearly bobbled the spoon when she realized it was Thad Law. But this wasn't the man in the rumpled suit that she'd met the previous day. This was a man in snug jeans and denim shirt with the sleeves rolled to his elbows, which displayed a toned, muscled body. She knew men in her parents' country club who worked out daily with personal trainers, hoping for a body like his.

In his arms was a cardboard box and a length of electrical wire.

Thad caught sight of her at the same moment and paused in mid-stride. Then he quickly recovered and walked closer. "'Morning."

"Good morning. I didn't expect to see you here this early."

He set down his burden on the bottom step and straightened, regarding her with that piercing look. "I might say the same for you."

She smiled easily. "I've always loved the morning." She nodded toward the cereal. "Have you had your breakfast?"

"Yeah." He arched a brow. "I didn't take you for the cereal type."

"Really? And what type did you think I'd be?"

"The eggs Benedict type, I guess. Or maybe the type that skips breakfast to leave room for quiche at lunch."

"Sorry to disappoint you." She spooned up the last of her cereal and set aside the bowl to stretch out her legs along the top step. "I made coffee. It's on the counter inside. Help yourself."

"Thanks." As he started up the steps she drew

her feet up to allow him to pass by. "As long as I'm pouring, would you like some?"

"Sure."

"Cream or sugar?"

"No thanks. I take it black."

He strode into the kitchen and returned minutes later with two cups of steaming coffee. Without a word he handed one to her.

He thought he'd prepared himself for that quick sizzle of heat, but it still managed to catch him by surprise when their fingers brushed.

He leaned his back against the rail and sipped in silence.

Heather sighed. "This is beautiful, isn't it?"

"Yeah." He sipped. Stared. And enjoyed the view. Not just the sunrise, but also the sight of the young woman who looked better in a shirt and jeans than anyone he'd ever seen. "Worth getting up early for."

Heather nodded toward the supplies. "What's all this for?"

"Some security devices I want added to your uncle's system."

"Are you going to install it yourself?"

He shook his head. "I have some workmen coming. I just wanted to check the system and make sure I had everything I needed before they get here. No point in wasting your uncle's time and money."

She shot him an astonished look.

He narrowed his eyes. "What?"

She shrugged. "I'm just a little surprised. Not too many people worry about someone else's money."

"I suppose such things don't matter to you." He saw her smile fade and wished he could take back his words.

"Of course they do. But he's my uncle. I figured you'd see him as just another rich guy in need of security, no matter what the price."

His voice lowered with temper. "Is that what you think of me?"

"Look, Thad." She got to her feet, coffee sloshing over the rim of her cup. "I don't know what to think. I came here to help my uncle. Apparently you did the same. So why don't you just do your job and ignore me."

As she started to sweep past him, his fingers closed around her upper arm and he dragged her close. "I wish I could. In fact, I'd really like to try. But I'm afraid it might prove impossible." His voice roughened. "I haven't figured you out yet, Heather McGrath. Yesterday you could have been the cover model for California Career Woman, all buttoned up in that tasteful little designer suit. This morning you look like a college student on mid-term break." His gaze swept her, from her bare toes to her ponytail, bringing high color to her cheeks. "Either way, I'm sure you're aware of the fact that it's impossible for a man not to notice you.''

He saw her eyes widen with surprise before narrowing to angry slits. It was the most fascinating thing to see. Even while her chin was lifting, he could almost feel her spine stiffening and white-hot fury seething through her veins.

''I don't care how you see me, or if you see me at all. If you value your job here, I suggest you take your hand off me immediately.''

He lowered his hand to his side, and marveled at the tingling in his fingertips. The mere touch of her had started a fire in his veins that was burning a path of heat directly to his loins.

She took a step back. ''Apparently you've decided to dislike me on principle. Maybe it's because I remind you of somebody. Or maybe I'm just a convenient target for some misplaced anger. Whatever the problem, Detective Law, it's yours, not mine. So deal with it. And in the meantime let's just keep out of each other's way.''

''I think that'd be wise.'' He reached down and took the cup from her hand.

At her arched brow he simply said, ''In your present state of mind, I'd hate to have you toss it at me. It's too hot.''

She almost laughed as he turned away and tossed

the coffee over the railing into some rosebushes, before carrying the cups to the kitchen.

By the time he returned, she'd walked to the far end of the porch and kept her back to him as he descended the steps and picked up his supplies.

As he walked away, a smile flitted across his lips. Damned if she wasn't just about irresistible when she got that temper up. He'd had all he could do to keep from dragging her against him and kissing those pouting lips.

It's a good thing he hadn't. A woman like that would probably go running to her uncle crying harassment. He'd had enough sensitivity training sessions to know a police officer had to hold himself to a higher standard.

Still, it hadn't been easy. There was just something about Heather McGrath that brought out the beast in him.

"A little higher." Thad stood on the ground, directing two workmen on ladders who were installing security cameras on the back of the house. Both would focus on the nearby hill. One lens gave a wide-angle view, the other a zoom, to be used for close-up shots of anyone trespassing.

In his hand was a palm-sized monitor showing what would appear on a much larger screen in Joe Colton's office.

"Okay. That's perfect." He switched off the monitor and was just turning away when he saw Heather and Joe coming across the lawn, heads bent close in earnest conversation.

He'd seen them go out earlier, and had assumed Joe's niece had talked him into taking her to town. Apparently they had just walked some of the property.

Joe was laughing. A rare sound these days. And a much-welcome one. Heather's answering laughter drifted on the breeze, as musical as fine wind chimes.

Until the two had gone out, they'd been locked in Joe's office all morning. Thad had only had to interrupt them once, to check the monitor. And when he had, he'd found Heather busy at the computer, a phone to her ear. Though she'd seen him, she hadn't acknowledged him in any way. But he'd seen her pass the phone to her uncle, before continuing with her work on the computer.

Maybe he'd been wrong about her. Maybe she actually did know how to work. For a day or two. He'd see just how disciplined she was after a little more time on the job.

In the meantime, he intended to heed her advice. He'd just keep his distance for a few days. By then she'd probably be gone. When the day came that he saw her toting a packed suitcase, he intended to remind her of their bet. Even spoiled little rich girls were required to pay when they lost. And that was one debt he'd enjoy collecting.

"Thad." Joe walked closer, trailed more slowly by his niece. "How's the work going?"

"Good. We should have these two cameras up and running soon and I'll show you how to switch them on and off from the console in your office."

"That's great." Joe looked up when the cell phone in Heather's pocket began ringing.

She turned away to answer it, then passed it to Joe. While he carried on an animated conversation with someone, Heather and Thad waited, an awkward silence stretching out between them.

"Time to get back to work," Joe announced as he handed the phone back to Heather. "I'll see you in my office whenever you're done here, Thad."

"Right." Thad watched as Heather walked away beside her uncle. She appeared relieved to be escaping. Not that he could blame her. He'd come across like a Neanderthal this morning.

There was just something about her that pushed all his buttons. And now that he'd had some time to consider, he knew why. She'd accused him of hating her on principle, because she reminded him of someone else. And she was right. Though she looked nothing like Vanessa, Heather came from the same privileged background as his late wife. He frowned as Heather and Joe disappeared inside the house. One broken heart was enough for any man. And the best way to ensure that it didn't happen again was to keep his distance. Which shouldn't be too hard, since Heather McGrath had already made it plain that she didn't want him around. Not that he minded. He already had so much going on in his life he found himself wishing he could be cloned.

A short time later he knocked on Joe's office door and stepped inside. The first thing he saw was Heather, standing on tiptoe trying to reach a leather-bound volume perched on a shelf high above her. Without thinking he strolled across the room and reached over her head, easily snagging the book. What he hadn't counted on was brushing her body with his. Or the way his body betrayed him without warning.

She turned with a smile. "Thanks, Uncle..." Her smile froze. "Thad."

"Sorry. I didn't mean to startle you again." He couldn't seem to look away from those soft blue eyes, wide with surprise. A man could easily drown in them. And happily go under without lifting a hand to save himself.

He lowered the book but didn't step away. He couldn't. He'd already fallen under the spell of her perfume. It was filling his lungs, clouding his mind.

He knew he was about to make a fool of himself,

but it didn't seem to matter. Nothing did at the moment except staying here, just like this, breathing her in and tempting himself with the thought of those lips.

She couldn't back up. There was nowhere to go. Her back was already firmly pressed to the bookcase. Besides, she wasn't sure she wanted to. The electricity sparking between them was mesmerizing. Like the static charge in the air before a wild summer storm.

She tipped her head higher. "If you're looking for my uncle, he should be back in a minute."

"Good. A minute's all I need for what I have in mind." Though an hour would have been better. Much better he thought as he lowered his face to hers.

Heather saw it coming and was helpless to stop it. But though she braced herself for his kiss, she was totally unprepared for what followed.

His free hand cupped the back of her head as his lips covered hers in a kiss so hot, so hungry, she was rocked back on her heels. This was no tentative brush of mouth to mouth, tasting, testing, persuading. This was all fire and flash and thunder. And she was tossed into the heart of the storm, with lightning flashing between them, and wildfires being ignited everywhere.

He crushed her against him and took the kiss

deeper. She could feel that hard, muscled body imprinting itself on hers. Branding her with his taste, his touch.

He kissed like a man who intended to possess her. She returned his kiss like a woman already possessed.

She was shocked by the way she was reacting. If any other man had dared to take such liberties, she would have cut him off at the knees with a single harsh word, a killing look, a slap across the face. But this man was kissing her breathless, and all she could do was hold on while her heart hitched, and her breathing became ragged, and her body, her flesh, her blood grew unbearably hot. She could feel her flesh melting. Her bones dissolving. Her blood singing in her veins. And her pulse pounding furiously in her ears.

Thad knew he'd crossed a line, both personal and professional, and yet he couldn't seem to stop. He needed, desperately, one more taste of her, one more touch. And so he lingered over her lips, struggling with an almost overwhelming desire to take her, here and now.

Even while the thought formed, he dismissed it as the cravings of a demented fool. Ever so slowly he lifted his head and watched as she struggled to compose herself.

Her eyes snapped open. Her lips, those soft, perfect lips, looked moist and swollen, still bearing the imprint of his. For some reason he couldn't fathom, that pleased him enormously.

"I'd like to say I'm sorry." He was surprised at how dry his throat felt. "But that would be a lie."

"All right. As long as we're being honest, I'd like to say I hate you for this." She could barely get the words out over the pressure in her throat. Her heart was still pumping furiously, her mind still clouded. "But I'm as much to blame as you."

"Well, then." He laid his palm against her cheek and saw her eyes go wide again. His smile was slow in coming, but when it did, it changed all his features. "Next time I'll let you kiss me first. Then we'll be even."

"Gee, thanks." But there was no anger in her tone. Only a hint of humor. She couldn't believe the change in him when he smiled. Those icy blue eyes warmed and heated. His mouth, so often set in hard tight lines, looked surprisingly soft. And there was a cleft in his chin she hadn't noticed before.

"You're welcome." Feeling stronger now, he took a step back, breaking contact.

He handed her the book. "I think this is what started all of that."

"Yes." She closed her hands around it, holding on to it like a lifeline, wondering if her heartbeat would ever return to normal.

He grinned. "My pleasure. If you ever need any more help reaching and fetching, just let me know."

They both looked up at the sound of footsteps. Joe stepped into his office and crossed to his desk. "Thad. I guess this means the cameras are installed?"

"Yeah. I thought I'd show you how to operate this monitor."

Heather remained where she was as Thad strolled to Joe's desk and the two men went over the controls.

After a few minutes Joe looked over at her. "You'd better learn these, too, sweetheart. As long as you'll be living here, you have to learn how to operate the security system."

"Yes, of course." She walked closer and was forced to endure the closeness of Thad's body as he explained the controls.

Each time he leaned forward to turn on another switch, she felt the sizzle of heat along her spine. And wondered if he felt it, too.

She chanced a quick glance at his face. He winked, and she felt her cheeks flame.

Finally, when she was certain she couldn't possibly endure being this close to him for another moment, he stepped back. "I think you've both got the hang of it."

"Well, if we have any questions, we'll know

where to find you." Joe began sorting through the mail on his desk, which Heather had already opened and stacked. He looked up as a thought occurred. "How about staying for dinner, Thad?"

"Sorry. I can't. I have…commitments."

"Okay. Maybe another time."

"Sure." Thad glanced at his watch, then started toward the door. "Sorry. I've got to run."

"Thanks for taking care of this, Thad. It's much appreciated."

Thad paused at the door and turned with a grin. "Don't say that until you get my bill. The Prosperino P.D. only pays me when I'm on duty. What I do for you goes on your tab."

Joe threw back his head and roared. "You're worth twice what you're charging me."

Thad grinned. "Now you tell me."

Joe waved a hand. "Will I see you tomorrow?"

"Yeah. But be warned. I'm going to be bringing you a list of security measures I think you should add."

"I've told you, Thad. I think the new cameras are enough."

"And I told you, not by a long shot. They're nothing but a stopgap measure. You ought to employ a security team until the shooter is behind bars."

"Uh-huh." Joe smiled. "See you tomorrow."

"Yeah." Thad shot a quick glance at Heather, standing beside her uncle's desk.

At once she felt the heat rise to her cheeks.

As the door closed behind him, she settled down to the computer and began scrolling until she found the figures she was searching for. But as she stared at the screen, the numbers blurred and she found herself replaying in her mind the kiss they'd shared.

She'd been kissed dozens of times. Hundreds. But she had never in her life felt anything that even came close to what she'd experienced with Thad Law.

What was happening here? She'd always considered herself a calm, intelligent, sensible woman. And yet, in the space of a single day, she felt as though her life had tilted at some crazy angle. As though she'd been caught up in something completely out of her realm of experience and totally out of her control.

Maybe it was just because Thad Law was unlike any of the men she'd ever known. Most of them were smooth-as-silk members of her family's country club, with a string of degrees after their names, eager to marry well and move up the corporate ladder. Most of them saw her as the perfect corporate wife.

Thad Law was about as far removed from that as a man could be. Tough talking, rough around the edges and completely unconcerned about how he ap-

peared to others. But she had the sense that he was
a man who would finish whatever he started, to the
best of his ability, come hell or high water. Maybe
that was why he so intrigued her. He appeared to be
that rarest of all breeds—a man of integrity.

And though it galled her to admit it, even to herself, she couldn't wait to see him again.

Three

The normally blue sky had turned to dull gunmetal gray. The sun had taken refuge behind dark clouds that gathered and thickened.

The family began drifting into the dining room. Heather stood with nine-year-old Joe, Jr., and seven-year-old Teddy, teasing them about the gloomy weather.

"Don't worry," Heather laughed. "You know what the song says. The sun'll come out tomorrow."

Both boys groaned and gave matching pained expressions before dissolving in laughter.

Their laughter faded when their mother entered.

It was clear to see that she was already well on her way to throwing a full-blown temper tantrum. Her eyes were as stormy as the clouds outside the windows. Her mouth a thin, tight line of anger.

As always she found fault with the way the table was set, with the flowers that had been carefully arranged as a centerpiece. She even found fault with the way Heather was dressed.

"This isn't a barn." Meredith looked her up and down without bothering to hide her contempt. "Save your denims and boots for the horses. I expect you to dress for dinner while you're a guest in my home."

It was on the tip of Heather's tongue to remind her aunt that this wasn't the White House, but one look at her two young cousins, and she felt a wave of sympathy. It must be terrible to have to live with so much seething anger and resentment. There seemed to be no love left in this home.

"If you'd like me to change…" she began.

"If I'd like?" Meredith's eyes narrowed to tiny slits. "Are you so thick-headed you have to ask? Get this straight. I don't want to see you in this room until you're wearing what you'd wear to one of your fancy country club dinners. Is that understood?"

Before Heather could reply Meredith slammed out of the room, leaving her sons staring after her in disbelief.

Hoping to calm them, Heather put an arm around each of them and gave them her brightest smile. "Looks like this is your lucky day. You're about to see me looking the way I look at a glamorous dinner party. I'll be right back after I change."

They all looked up at the sound of a loud report, followed by the shattering of glass.

"What was that?" Teddy's eyes went wide with fear.

Even as he cried out the question, they all knew what they'd heard. It was unmistakably a gunshot. The sound was eerily like the sound they'd heard another time, at Joe's party.

For the space of a heartbeat they all went perfectly still, absorbing the shock.

Heather was the first to recover her senses. She was already rushing through the open doorway and toward the stairs, a scream lodged in her throat, when the boys started after her. Seeing them, she stopped and held out her hands.

"You don't want to come up here," she said insistently. "Not until I see what's happened."

The thought of these two little boys finding their father lying in a pool of blood, dead or wounded, was too terrible to contemplate. As they rushed toward her she caught them and held them back, then glanced over their heads to where Inez stood in the doorway, staring in stunned silence. "Take the boys with you into the dining room and keep them there.''

The poor woman was too frightened to respond.

Just then her aunt hurried into the hallway.

The woman who had for years pretended to be Meredith paused at the scene before her. Her mind couldn't seem to take in what her heart already knew. The gunshot. The eerie silence. It was so much like the previous time. But that time she'd been prepared. It had all been carefully choreographed by her, Patsy Portman. This time the gunshot had caught her completely by surprise. What was going on here? This hadn't been part of her plan. In fact, she'd been so busy trying to do away with Emily, she hadn't given any more thought to getting rid of Joe.

''Aunt Meredith.'' Seeing her aunt's apparent confusion, Heather adopted a tone she'd used as a camp counselor whenever she was dealing with an errant child. ''You don't want your boys to go up here. Please see that they stay downstairs, out of harm's way.''

For a few more seconds Patsy's mind seemed to be somewhere else, mulling this strange twist. Then, with great effort, she pulled herself back from her thoughts and called sternly, ''You heard Heather. Come down here and wait with me.''

Heather turned away, relieved, and started up. Just

then Joe Colton appeared at the head of the stairs. In his eyes was a look of dazed fury.

In a voice that sounded deadly calm he said, "Heather, call the police."

"Are you all right? Was it a gunshot?"

He nodded. "I'm fine. Call now. And, Heather…"

She paused.

"Keep everyone downstairs and in one place until the police detectives have had a chance to gather evidence. We know the routine by now. I don't want anyone messing up footprints or other signs this madman may have left behind."

She was so grateful to see that her uncle was alive and unharmed, she could hardly speak. She gave a quick nod of her head, then raced toward the phone. After speaking with the police, she realized that she was trembling. Joining the others in the dining room she sank down onto a chair and waited for the tremors to pass.

Thad Law was out of his car and striding across the yard within minutes of the call. He was thankful that he'd been in the vicinity. Otherwise there was no telling how long it might have taken him.

As he drew near the front door he saw a shadowy figure and drew his gun.

"Police. Hold it right there." He saw the figure

pause and dart a look toward him. At that same moment he took careful aim. "I wouldn't move if I
were you, unless you'd like this to be your last minute on earth."

The voice was low and deep and slightly out of
breath. "What the hell is this about?"

"I'll ask the questions." Thad could see the man
clearly outlined in the spill of light from the glass
panels on either side of the door. His shrewd cop's
mind was already memorizing every detail. A hair
over six feet. Strong, rugged build. Jet black hair.
Dressed casually enough, in charcoal slacks and
sweater. To blend into the darkness? Thad wondered.

He stepped closer and spun the man around, forcing his face to the door, while he searched for a
weapon. Seeing that he wasn't armed, Thad stepped
back, allowing the man to turn.

Thad's tone was sharp. "Now tell me who you
are and what you're doing here."

The man looked startled by the questions before
saying, "My name's Jackson Colton. I'm here to see
my uncle."

"You got a beef with Joe Colton?"

"A beef? Of course not. I'm Joe's nephew, and
I'm here for a visit."

"Did Joe know you were coming?"

There was a slight hesitation before Jackson said

quietly, "No. I didn't call and tell him I was coming. With Joe it isn't necessary. His family is always welcome. Now I'd like to know what right you have to hold me at gunpoint and ask me these questions."

"I have every right. There were shots fired here." Thad gave a sharp rap on the door and waited until it was opened by a trembling Inez. Shoving Jackson ahead of him, he headed toward Joe Colton's office. As he stepped inside he heard the high-pitched wail of sirens signaling the arrival of the rest of the squad. When a uniform rushed into the room, Thad nodded his head toward Jackson Colton.

"This guy claims to be a relative. He was outside when I got here. See that he sits in that chair and doesn't move until I've had a chance to interview everyone here." He gave Jackson a look that spoke, more than any words, what would happen if he dared to argue.

Then he was gone, his face as dark as a thundercloud.

Heather sat with Teddy and Joe, Jr., while uniformed men swarmed over the area, bagging everything that seemed the least bit suspicious. While one team went over every inch of the grounds directly surrounding the house, another team worked inside, checking doors, windows, locks. The master suite was sealed off while a team sifted through every shard of broken glass.

Inez had been ordered to stay until a statement could be taken from her. Joe and Meredith were closed in the great room with Thad Law and several detectives, answering questions.

"Heather." Joe, Jr., looked grave in the lamp-light. "Why does somebody want to kill my dad?"

"I don't know, honey." She wrapped her arm around the boy, offering him what comfort she could. "I wish I knew. I guess there will always be people in this world who want to hurt other people."

"Why can't the police arrest all the bad people?" Teddy's blue eyes were troubled.

"They try, Teddy. They do the best they can. But before they can arrest somebody, they have to find out who he is. That's why they're talking to every-body who was here tonight. To see if any of us can help them find the bad people. And believe me, Teddy, if it's at all possible, I believe the police will find the person who did this."

"Heather's right about that."

At the sound of Thad Law's voice, their heads came up.

Heather wondered just how long he'd been stand-ing there, watching and listening. As a detective, he would have been trained to listen and observe. But this seemed to be more than training. It seemed almost second nature to him. As though he'd spent a lifetime looking into people's minds and probing the secrets of their hearts.

Thad closed the door and leaned against it. "If you boys don't mind, I'd like to ask you a favor."

The two boys' fears were forgotten as they wondered what they could possibly do for this man, who was held in such high regard by their father.

He crossed to the two little boys and got down on his knees, so that his eyes were level with theirs. It occurred to Heather as she watched that he was doing everything possible to make himself less intimidating. He instinctively understood that his size, his bearing, and his status as a police detective, could be misinterpreted as menacing.

"I need to learn everything I can about the past couple of hours." He turned to the older boy first. "What were you doing when you heard the sound of the gunshot, Joe?"

"That's easy," Joe, Jr., said solemnly. "We were in the dining room, waiting for our dad to join us for dinner."

"Were you sitting at the table?" Thad turned to the younger boy.

Teddy shook his head. "We were standing."

"Alone?"

The boy shook his head. "With Heather." He glanced tentatively toward her and was relieved to see her smiling. His own smile returned. "She was teasing us."

"Teasing you? What about?" He glanced over the boy's head and saw the color rise to Heather's cheeks.

"About the clouds. She told us the sun'll come out tomorrow."

Thad grinned. "Did she say it? Or sing it?"

"She said it. But in a singsong voice." The little boy was clearly enjoying himself now that he'd discovered that the policeman had a sense of humor.

"Okay. As long as she didn't burst into song." Thad kept his tone light. "Then what happened?"

"Our mom came in and yelled at Heather." Teddy saw the look of disapproval on his brother's face and clapped a hand to his mouth. "Maybe I wasn't supposed to tell."

"That's all right," Thad said easily. "My mom used to yell sometimes, too. Moms do that. What did she yell about?"

"She told Heather not to come to the table in jeans. And Heather was just going to go and change when we heard the bang."

"Were you all together when you heard the sound?"

The boy nodded, then paused. "Well, I guess our mom wasn't here." He turned to his brother for confirmation. "She ran out of the room a minute or so before Heather."

"So there were only the three of you?"

Teddy nodded. "And Inez."

"All right." Thad kept his tone easy. "After your mother left, what did you say and do?"

Teddy grinned, remembering. "Heather said we were lucky, 'cause she was going upstairs to make herself glamorous."

"And did she?"

Teddy shook his head. "Before she could go we heard the shot. Bam. Then Heather ran out of the room and started up the stairs. And when Joe and I tried to follow, she told us to stay downstairs."

Thad nodded. "That was very wise of her. And then what happened next?"

"Heather called to Inez to take us back to the dining room. But she was too scared. And then our mom came along, but before she could take us away, our dad came to the top of the stairs and told Heather to call the police. And he told us all to stay out of the way while the police did their job."

"Good." Thad patted both boys on the shoulders. "You all did the right thing."

As he got to his feet Joe, Jr., tipped up his head. "Did you find the man who fired the shot?"

"I can't say, son."

"But you'll catch him, won't you?"

Thad touched a hand to the boy's shoulder, hearing so much more than the mere question. It was the underlying fear. A fear that would dog all of them until the shooter was identified and arrested. Whether awake or asleep, the little nagging thought would always be in the back of their minds. They weren't safe. Even in their own home, they could find no refuge from this stalker until he was taken into custody and locked behind bars for his crime.

"You can count on it, son."

At that both boys looked greatly relieved.

Teddy asked, "Are you going to stay here with us until he's caught?"

Thad shook his head. "I'm afraid that isn't possible. But I'll see that you get all the security that's available."

Joe, Jr., dropped an arm around his younger brother's shoulders. "Can we go up to our rooms now?"

Thad nodded. "Yeah. Your mom will be right with you."

The two boys hurried away, leaving Thad and Heather alone.

She took a deep breath. "Tell me what you've found."

He shook his head. "First tell me what you saw, what you heard, and anything that the boys might have left out."

"Basically, what the boys told you is all there was."

"They didn't leave anything out?"

She shook her head. "It caught us all by surprise. I think we're still a little stunned by it." She clutched her hands together tightly to control the shaking. Now that the danger was past, she was suffering from the shock of what might have been. "Is my uncle all right?"

"He's fine. The window in his bedroom is shattered. Apparently the shooter was down below, saw him by the window, and took his shot, not knowing that in that instant Joe was reaching for his shoes. If he hadn't bent down at that very moment, we might be investigating a murder instead of just an attempted murder."

He saw the way her face drained of color. Though he wanted to offer her some comfort, he knew better. He was a detective investigating a serious crime. He couldn't afford to lose his concentration. Or his objectivity. And this woman was capable of robbing him of both with a single touch.

"What can you tell me about Jackson Colton?"

Her eyes widened. "Jackson? He's Joe's nephew. His brother's son. Why do you want to know about Jackson?"

"He was here at the time of the shooting. I came upon him just as I arrived."

"Jackson is here?" She glanced toward the door. "Where is he?"

"Being questioned."

"But why?"

Thad struggled to remain patient. "Because he arrived unannounced at the precise time that shots were fired by an unknown gunman. He's alone, and has no one who can provide him with an alibi for the time of the shooting."

"You think that Jackson…?" She couldn't bring herself to speak the words. "No. This is insane."

Thad gave a sigh of impatience. "Do you know of anyone who would want Joe Colton dead?"

Heather closed her eyes a moment as the enormity of the situation washed over her. Then she opened them and shook her head. "No. I'm sure he's made a few enemies during his lifetime. But for a man to want another man dead?" She let out a long, slow sigh. "I can't even conceive of such a thing."

That was, he realized, the biggest difference between them. Not money or lifestyles or goals. It was the fact that she couldn't even conceive of such a man, while he had spent every day of the past ten years coming into contact with such men and trying to make some sense of the destruction they brought to innocent victims.

"Maybe it's time you thought about going back home," he said wearily.

"Leave my uncle just when he needs me most?"

"Look, Heather. This isn't a video game of virtual bad guys. This is deadly serious. Someone wants Joe Colton dead. It could very well be a member of his own family." He thought again about the timing of Jackson Colton's arrival. "And very often, when you have a madman loose with a gun, innocent people get caught in the crossfire. So my best advice to you is to leave Prosperino now and go back where you belong."

Where you belong.

The words hung between them for the space of a heartbeat.

Heather's eyes went wide before narrowing with anger. "Thanks for the warning. I'm sure you mean well. But I have no intention of leaving Uncle Joe alone. Especially now."

"He would understand. I'm sure—"

She crossed to the door, cutting off whatever else he was about to say. "Are you through with me, Detective? Because if you are, I'd really like to go and talk to my uncle now."

Thad clenched his jaw. "Yeah. We're through. For now."

As she yanked open the door and walked away it occurred to him that she was definitely going to be a problem. How the hell was he supposed to do his job without worrying about her?

He muttered a couple of rich, ripe oaths as he realized that Heather McGrath was the most damnably obstinate female he'd ever met.

And, like an itch he couldn't scratch, she was taking up entirely too much of his valuable time.

"I'm fine, Dad." Heather sat on the edge of her bed and spoke into the cell phone. "Tell Mom that Uncle Joe has already added more security cameras and is hiring a security firm to patrol the grounds. I overheard him telling the police detective that he'll do whatever it takes to keep his family safe until this gunman is found."

She listened, then waited while she could hear her father passing the phone to her mother. She spoke quietly with Andie McGrath before saying, "We had this same argument before I left San Diego. I know you're worried, and will continue to worry, but I'll be fine. And I promise to phone regularly. Please understand I'm feeling useful here. I think being here with Uncle Joe has made a difference. We're working our way through a mountain of paperwork. And that helps relieve some of his stress." She paused, listened, then added, "I love you, Mom. Tell Dad I love him, too."

She set down the phone and walked to her bedroom window to stare at the figures of the police officers silhouetted in the moonlight.

One figure stood out from all the others. One tall, muscular man standing in the grass, staring up at Joe Colton's window.

Suddenly his head turned slightly and she realized he was looking up at her, and that she was clearly outlined in the overhead light.

Naked. Vulnerable. Just as her uncle had been, before the bullet had pierced his window.

She watched a moment longer, then stepped away and turned out the light.

As she crawled into bed it felt oddly comforting to know that Thad Law was there, looking out for their safety. There was such strength in him. Not just physical strength, though that was apparent. She sensed something else in him. A goodness, a determination, a strength of will, that made her believe he would accomplish whatever task he set for himself. Without regard to the obstacles or the dangers, he would put himself in the line of fire for those charged to his care.

What sort of man willingly chose such a task? What quality was there in Thad Law that he would risk his own life for the lives of complete strangers? She thought about the men she knew. Most of them were well-educated, but absolutely lacking in any sort of street smarts. They knew how to climb the corporate ladder, would pay any price for the right clothes, the right haircut, the right image. But if they found their lives in danger, they would be thrust into a state of panic.

She couldn't imagine any situation that would send Thad Law ducking and hiding. He was the type who would stand tall against an enemy, no matter how much danger it entailed.

It wasn't the badge or the gun that impressed her about Detective Law. It was the man himself. He struck her as one who would be absolutely fearless in the face of any threat.

She sensed a darkness in him. A determination to get the job done against all odds, without regard to personal safety.

There was such comfort in that.

She fell asleep, secure in the knowledge that, at least for tonight, no harm would come to them while their dark guardian angel was looking out for them.

Four

"I have your conference call arranged, Uncle Joe." Heather handed over the phone.

"Thanks, sweetheart." Joe Colton shifted in his chair, his hand over the receiver. "You've put in enough hours today. When I'm through with this, I'm calling it a day. You know you've been dying to go horseback riding. Why not now?"

She brushed a kiss over his forehead. "I like the way you think. Sure you don't want me to wait and you can join me?"

He shook his head. "It may be a bit cool, but I intend to take myself out to the pool and do laps before dinner."

"Okay. It's a good thing it's heated." She waved as she headed out of his office.

A short time later, dressed in boots and denims, her hair tucked under a baseball cap, she started toward the stable.

It was one of those perfect California days. A clear, cloudless sky with sunlight so bright it hurt to look at it. The air, as she drew closer to the stables, was ripe with dung and freshly turned earth. She breathed it in, as comfortable here as she would be at a country club dance.

Heather loved riding. From the time she'd been a little girl she'd had a passion for horses. And though her parents had expressed concern about her recklessness, she'd refused to give it up.

Now, for the next few hours, she would indulge herself.

She stepped inside the stable and waited for her eyes to adjust. After the brilliant sunlight outside, it seemed almost gloomy as she made her way between the rows of stalls.

Suddenly she heard a deep familiar voice muttering a rich, ripe oath. She looked up to see Thad Law standing on a ladder, fiddling with a security camera. In the heat of the barn he'd removed his shirt and tossed it in the dirt below. Her heart did a series of flips at the sight of his naked back and arms, rippling with muscles.

She'd seen him for days, going over the security system with a team of professionals. But she had the strong suspicion that he'd been avoiding her.

Just then he tightened a switch and security lights flashed on, indicating that the sensors had detected an intruder. He turned and caught sight of Heather looking up at him.

His frown slowly dissolved. "Sorry. Guess I didn't hear you."

"That's all right, Detective Law. I'm just getting even for those times you've managed to catch me by surprise."

He climbed down the ladder and picked up his shirt, mopping sweat from his face and chest before slipping his arms into the sleeves. While he buttoned it, Heather couldn't seem to tear her gaze from the mat of dark hair on his chest.

He tucked the ends of his shirt into his waistband. "Did your uncle send for me?"

She shook her head. "He didn't even mention that you were here. I was just going to ride." She glanced at the new security camera. "Do you really think that's necessary in here?"

He arched a brow. "Do you have any idea how much all this horseflesh is worth? Not to mention the building. If someone wanted to hurt Joe Colton, setting fire to the stable might be a good start."

Heather couldn't keep the pained expression from

her eyes. "It's hard to believe anyone could do such a cruel thing to helpless animals."

"Believe it." He saw the look in her eyes and felt a rush of annoyance. Not at her, but at himself for putting it there. His job had hardened him to the violence man was capable of. He was sure a woman like Heather McGrath, raised in that ivory tower, didn't have a clue.

"Anyone who can fire a shot during a crowded party has no conscience. A man, a horse, or half a dozen innocent bystanders. It's all the same to a cold-blooded killer."

She shivered and wondered if Thad knew how fierce he looked when he talked about lawbreakers. If ever she'd doubted his passion, she needed only to hear his words and look into his eyes to see the depth of it. She wouldn't want to cross this man's path on the wrong side of the law.

He glanced around. "Which horse are you planning to ride?"

"Diablo."

At that Thad's eyes narrowed. "Joe told me he's the toughest stallion in his stable."

She nodded. "That may be. But he and I are well suited. We both enjoy speed and the freedom to leave the well-worn trails and just run where the mood takes us."

"I'd rather you'd stick to the trails, if you don't mind."

She was about to argue when she recognized the thread of steel behind those softly spoken words. She gave a careless shrug. "Okay."

She crossed to the stallion's stall and lifted a hand to its nose, giving Diablo a chance to get her scent. The horse blew and snorted as she opened the door and stepped inside.

Thad walked closer to watch as she expertly tossed a blanket over the horse's back, and then a saddle, which she quickly cinched. When she lifted the bridle, Diablo tossed his head, but with a few soft words she managed to calm him enough to take the bit.

Thad seemed surprised to see the ease with which she saddled her own mount. "I figured you'd want somebody to do that for you."

She shook her head. "As an equestrienne you handle your own equipment, so if there's any problem with it you have nobody else to blame. That's the first rule. The second rule is, see to your horse's needs. That means a good rubdown when you're through, followed by a check of the feed and water, before going off to take a shower."

He grinned. "With just a few words changed, the same rules apply for being a good cop."

She paused, considering, then nodded. "I never

thought about it before. But you're right. I'm sure you always have to put the public ahead of your own needs."

"And I never trust anyone but myself to inspect my equipment. If my gun should misfire, it's nobody's fault but mine."

She had no doubt that he would treat his gun with the same care that he seemed to treat all the security devices here on her uncle's property.

Minutes later she opened the stall door and led the stallion out into the sunshine.

She turned to where Thad was standing. "Sure you don't want to join me?"

He shook his head. "I still have some work to do in here. Then I'll have to check the monitor, and show your uncle which switch will control the stable cameras."

"That's too bad. It's the perfect day for a ride." Her smile was quick and sly. "And maybe we could have made another bet. Which I'd no doubt win."

He watched as she pulled herself up to the saddle and dug her heels into Diablo's sides. The horse took off at a fast clip, its hooves spewing dirt.

As horse and rider headed across the rolling meadow, Thad stood for the longest time, enjoying the view. Damned if Heather McGrath wasn't just about the prettiest thing he'd ever seen. Especially on the back of such a magnificent animal.

The absurdity of it suddenly struck him. He was watching an angel riding a devil. If he had to bet which one held the upper hand, his money was on the angel.

"I've had light sensors mounted front and back, and cameras installed inside the stable." Standing beside Joe's desk, Thad threw several switches. "Anyone who gets within ten feet of the building will cause the lights to go on. Once inside, you can view them here..." He switched on a camera to show an overview of the horses in their stalls. "...and close up like this." He flicked another switch and directed the zoom lens, catching a mare in the act of eating hay.

"You do good work, Thad. Why, I can even zoom in on the fly buzzing around her ear." Joe looked up at the ringing of his phone. "Excuse me a minute."

He swiveled his chair and reached for a file while he spoke into the phone.

Thad studied the monitors and caught sight of Heather and Diablo just cresting a hill. He stared at it for long seconds. Then, glancing at Joe's bent head, he threw a second switch directing the close-up camera toward Heather's face. The sight of her, laughing as the wind took her baseball cap and sent her hair fanning out around her, had him watching with avid interest.

She slowed the horse, touching the reins to his neck until he turned. When they reached the spot where her cap had landed, she leaned low in the saddle, snatching up her hat as the horse's hooves pounded the earth.

Thad held his breath for a moment, afraid she would surely fall and be trampled. Instead she straightened and flicked the reins, urging the horse once more into a run.

She looked so easy and comfortable astride the big black stallion. Whatever tension she displayed when she was around Thad had disappeared. In its place was grace and poise. Natural beauty. If a film-maker were to catch this on video, he could market it without a single sound in the background. All that was needed to hold the viewer's attention was the woman, the horse, and the rolling hills of Prosper-ino.

Joe set aside the phone and turned. The first thing he noticed was the rapt expression on Thad's face. Then he glanced at the monitor and saw the close-up of his niece.

"She's beautiful, isn't she?"

Thad nodded, afraid to trust his voice.

"The best thing of all about Heather is that she's as sweet, as good-hearted as she is lovely to look at. But then, I'm sure you've discovered that for yourself."

"I...haven't had time to notice much of anything, Joe." Just then he caught sight of Jackson Colton on the monitor, urging his Palomino into a gallop to catch up with Heather.

Thad's smile faded. His frown deepened. "Now, about the new security in the stables."

For the next hour he and Joe went over the controls until Joe felt comfortable with everything that had been added.

Finally the older man pushed away from his desk. "Is that everything?"

Thad nodded.

"Good. Now, since you're off the clock, how about a drink?"

Thad glanced at his watch. "Sorry. I have to get back to town."

"You're a hard man to pin down, Thad. Could I persuade you to stay for dinner if I told you Inez was fixing sirloin tips in wine sauce?"

Thad gave a rare grin. "That's tempting, Joe. But between the police department and the extra hours here, I'm running as fast as I can."

"Yeah. I understand. I'm sure you need a little time for a personal life as well."

Thad's smile faded. "A schedule like mine doesn't leave time for a life."

"Then you've got to make time, man." Joe clapped a hand on his shoulder. "I've got spare swim trunks in the pool house. Sure you can't join me?"

"You're making it awfully tempting."

"When was the last time you took a couple of hours just for yourself?"

Thad thought a minute. "Probably three years ago. When I was recovering from a gunshot wound."

Both men laughed.

Joe tried one last argument. "Heather will probably be back soon, and I'm sure we can persuade her to join us as well."

Thad nearly weakened at the thought of seeing Heather in a bathing suit. Then he squared his shoulders. "Sorry, Joe. I just can't spare the time."

As he made his way to his car Thad thought about all the demands being made on his time. He felt he was being stretched to the very limit. Still... He paused, and glanced toward the stables. What he wouldn't give to spend a lazy evening around the pool, doing nothing more strenuous than lifting a drink to his lips.

And, of course, watching Heather McGrath in a bathing suit. A bikini, he decided as he turned the ignition and started away from the ranch. Better yet, a thong. Bright pink.

He was grinning as he let his imagination take him where he had no doubt reality would never permit him to go.

It wasn't pink. And it wasn't a thong, or even a bikini. It was a plain black tank.

Thad paused in mid-stride and stared in pure male appreciation when, days later, he caught sight of Heather poised on the high board. With that fabulous body, that sun-bronzed skin and all that honey hair, she was absolutely riveting. She lifted her hands above her head, took one quick bounce on the board before soaring through the air and cutting neatly into the water.

She was, he realized, pure poetry in motion.

She broke the water and tossed her head, sending her hair fanning out around her shoulders like a veil of glistening diamonds. Then she began to swim in smooth, long strokes until she reached the edge of the pool, where she pulled herself out and reached for a towel.

She was still drying herself when she turned and saw Thad walking toward her. He'd removed his suit jacket and rolled the sleeves of his white shirt. His eyes were hidden behind reflecting sunglasses.

She smiled. "I didn't know you'd be here today."

"Neither did I. But I had some questions for your

uncle. And I thought I'd see how the sensors were working in the stable before I head home.''

"Do you ever take a day off?"

He slipped off the glasses and Heather absorbed a jolt at the heat of his gaze. "No. And for once I'm glad. Tell me, do you swim every day after work?"

"Not always. Some days I ride. Other days I just walk over the hills until it's time for dinner. Why?"

"I figured if I could count on seeing you like this at the same time every day, I'd make it a point to be here. Strictly as an impartial observer, you understand, to see to your safety."

His unexpected humor had her laughing. A clear sound that did something to his heart. "Of course. I didn't realize you were so noble, Detective Law."

"Yeah. That's me. Pure of mind and brave of heart." Reluctantly he turned away. "I guess I'd better get over to the stable."

"I'll walk with you."

He halted. "I don't think you'd like to walk barefoot. That is unless you don't mind stepping in some pretty slimy stuff."

She stepped into a pair of drawstring pants and slipped her feet into canvas deck shoes. "If I encounter any 'slimy stuff,' I'll just toss these in the washer."

As he moved along beside her he said, "I figured you'd have a maid looking after your stuff."

"I take care of my own stuff, as you call it. I didn't come here for a vacation. I came here to lend a hand to my Uncle Joe."

"I thought I heard somebody mention my name." Joe Colton came around the side of the house, accompanied by his nephew Jackson, and offered his hand to Thad. "Have you finally found a chance to join us for dinner?"

"Sorry. No. I just stopped by to check the sensors in the stable. How have they been working?"

Joe shrugged. "Fine. Although Heather set off the alarm once." He turned to his niece. "Did you tell him?"

She shook her head. "I feel silly mentioning it." She glanced at Thad. "I forgot about the new alarm code and just started saddling Diablo. The next thing I knew I had Uncle Joe and half a dozen security people swarming all over the place."

Joe started laughing as he recalled the scene. "I don't know who looked more scared—Heather, Diablo or our security team."

Thad's smile was immediately gone. "Your security team looked scared?"

"Hey." Joe attempted to smooth it over. "This was their first encounter with the alarm. They're green, Thad. And still thinking about the shot fired through my window. Maybe scared was the wrong term. They looked like they'd been caught by surprise.''

''All the more reason why they should have behaved like professionals.'' Thad's eyes were narrowed in thought as he continued on toward the stable. After checking the sensors, and testing the alarm, he stepped out into the fading sunshine.

''If you'd like, Joe, I could give you the names of a couple of security firms that we've worked with in the past.''

Joe thought about it, then shook his head. ''I'll keep the ones I hired. But I'd feel a whole lot better if you'd take over as head of the team.''

Thad didn't bother to hide his impatience. ''Thanks, Joe. I'm flattered that you'd think I could make a difference. But I've already got more on my plate than I can handle. And I'm beginning to think that what you need is a full-time bodyguard.''

He could see the effect his words had on Joe and his niece. He slipped on his sunglasses. ''Sorry, Joe. I'm not trying to be an alarmist. It's just my training to always imagine the worst-case scenario. You've got enough to worry about without having me add to your burden.'' He stuck out his hand. ''I have to go now. Let me know if you want the names of other security firms.''

''Yeah.'' Joe accepted his handshake.

Thad nodded toward Jackson, then glanced at

Heather's face and could see the worried look in her eyes. He hated that he'd had to be the one to put such fear in her. Still, she needed to know that life wasn't always a walk in the park.

As he made his way to his car he found himself wishing he could call back the last half hour. Even though he knew better than to keep tempting himself, he'd have indulged his fantasies by staying in the shadows a whole lot longer while watching Heather swim.

It wouldn't do anything to help his investigation, which seemed to be going nowhere. But spending a few extra minutes treating his senses to Heather McGrath in a revealing bathing suit would go a long way toward soothing his soul and improving his dreams.

Five

Patsy stared at the rain streaking the windows, her mood as gloomy as the weather. It had been raining for three straight days. She was sick of it.

When the housekeeper walked by, Patsy stopped her. "Where are you supposed to be right now?"

Inez looked bewildered. "Cleaning the courtyard, Mrs. Colton. But the rain—"

"Then do it. That's what you're being paid to do. How many times do I have to tell you? I don't want you underfoot."

The woman fled.

Patsy watched her go while her anger continued

to fester. This weather made her antsy. The isolation of this place was getting to her, closing in on her. She was sick of people tiptoeing around her. Tired of Inez always making Joe's favorite meals. What about hers?

Joe. Her frown deepened. She'd been so busy trying to locate Emily, she hadn't been paying any attention to her plot to do away with Joe. Now there'd been another attempt on his life, and that detective was here, sniffing around. She hated him. Hated those long, probing looks. Like he already knew who and what she was and was just waiting for her to make one little mistake.

He'd been asking all kinds of questions. And every time she answered one, he had two more.

She knew his kind. He was trying to trip her up. She needed to get out of here. Away from Joe. He and Heather McGrath were constantly closeting themselves up in his office, completely shutting her out.

She started to pace. How had Meredith been able to tolerate this for so many years?

Meredith. The mere thought of her had Patsy pausing, a ghost of a smile on her lips. She was Meredith now and she would do whatever she pleased.

She picked up a phone and made her plans, then

stalked toward Joe's office. Without bothering to knock, she tore open the door and stared around.

Heather was seated at the computer, her fingers flying over the keys. Joe was across the room, engaged in an animated conversation. From the few words she overheard, Patsy realized that he was on a conference call with several of the executives of Colton Enterprises.

Joe looked up and seeing her, said softly, "Excuse me, gentlemen." With a hand over the receiver he turned to his wife. "Is there a problem?"

Patsy was actually disappointed to find Joe and Heather hard at work. It would have been such fun to find them looking a little too cozy with one another. She could have gotten a lot of mileage out of such a scene.

Her tone was brittle. "I can't stand being cooped up here. I've made an appointment at LaBelle."

Recognizing the name of one of the most exclusive spas in California, Joe uttered a sound of disgust. "That's more than a hundred miles from here."

"Everything's almost a hundred miles from here." Her voice took on the whining tone that had become so familiar. "I don't know when I'll be back. I've decided I need a few days of pampering."

With a toss of her head she walked away, slamming the door. Minutes later her car roared down the drive.

Heather watched as her uncle returned to the phone. No tender kiss goodbye for these two, she thought. Or even a smile from across the room. Whatever had once brought them such joy was long ago lost and apparently forgotten.

It made her sad. Joe Colton was such a good man, and there had been a time when she'd thought Meredith Colton was his perfect soul mate. Apparently there had been too many years and too many tears between them. The death of a son and the disappearance of a daughter had been difficult enough to bear. Now the rift seemed to widen with every passing day, until this second attempt on Joe's life was just another burden heaped upon his shoulders.

A short time later Joe's frown was replaced by a smile when the sun suddenly burst through the clouds. When a knock sounded on the door, it opened to reveal Thad Law.

"Well." Joe beckoned him in. "Did you bring this sunshine with you?"

"Sorry. I wish I could claim the credit, but it's not in my realm of expertise."

Thad glanced from Joe to Heather. He resented the fact that she'd been on his mind far too much these past days. Images of her riding Diablo or just walking calmly across the lawn, intruded at the strangest times. When he was bogged down in paperwork. When he was interrogating a witness. Even while he was sleeping. Especially then. She seemed always to be tiptoeing across his heart.

"How's the investigation coming along?"

Thad shrugged. "About the same as before." He refused the chair Joe indicated, choosing instead to stand as he gave Joe one of those measuring looks. "You've made your share of enemies, Joe."

"You mean the list has grown longer? Whose name have you added now?"

Thad glanced at Heather, then back to Joe. "Nobody new. Just the same old names. But it isn't easy checking out every one of them." He cleared his throat, obviously uncomfortable. "But I wonder if your wife would be willing to sit down and talk with me about some of your mutual friends."

Joe met the detective's steady look. "Meredith's gone out of town for a couple of days. But when she returns you can try to arrange it."

Before Thad could respond, Joe was quick to add, "I'm not saying she'll agree, you understand. My wife is free to make her own decisions about this."

Thad nodded. "Okay. I understand. I'll call in a couple of days and talk to her."

Joe studied the tight line of Thad's mouth. "Do you suspect one of our guests?"

"Everybody's a suspect, Joe. You know that. I keep going over the whereabouts of every guest at the time the shot was fired. And now I'm trying to tie a suspect from the first shooting to this latest one."

"So you think one of our guests slipped away and fired that first shot?"

Thad shook his head. "I didn't say that. But there are only two theories. Either it was a guest with a grudge, or it was a hired assassin. Either way, until the shooter is found, you're not out of the woods."

As he turned away Joe called, "Is that all you came here for?"

Thad turned back. "Yeah. I thought I'd take a chance on catching your wife. And I wanted you to know how the investigation is going."

"Then, since you have a little time anyway, why not stay for dinner?"

Even as the detective was shaking his head, Joe was getting to his feet. "Heather and I have been cooped up for days doing nothing but paperwork. I'll bet you've been doing the same."

"I have but—"

Joe held up a hand to stop him. "Okay, then. It's time to relax. Which do you prefer? Riding or a cold beer in the courtyard?"

Thad laughed. "Personally a cold beer sounds best to me."

"You're on." Joe turned to Heather. "That sound you hear is the five o'clock whistle, young lady. You have one minute to shut down your computer and join Thad and me out in the courtyard."

"Yes, sir." With a laugh Heather inserted a disk and began to back up her work.

Minutes later she found Joe and Thad already seated by the fountain, drinking beer.

Joe looked up. "What'll you have, sweetheart?"

"The same as you."

Thad watched as she settled herself on a chaise across from him. She tucked her feet under her as she accepted a frosty mug from her uncle.

As Joe turned away, Thad said softly, "I figured you for the champagne and cavier type."

"I can be, when the situation calls for it. But there are times when nothing tastes better than a cold beer." She smiled at her uncle. "Especially after the work we managed to accomplish today."

Joe winked at her as he chose a cushioned chair. "You've turned out an amazing amount of work since you got here. I think if you stay long enough, you just might dig me out from under that mountain that's had me buried."

She gave a nod of acknowledgment. "My pleasure, sir. That's what I'm here for."

Joe turned to Thad. "See why I love her?"

Thad ducked his head and sipped his beer. He

wondered just what the hell he was doing here. He was being paid to investigate not one, but two attempts on Joe Colton's life. And here he was drinking with the intended victim and thinking things he had no right to about the victim's niece.

He glowered as Jackson Colton entered the courtyard and joined them. It occurred to Thad that this man might very well be the snake in the Garden of Eden. Right now he was number one on the list of suspects.

Still, the music of the fountain and the coolness of the courtyard and the soothing sound of Heather's velvet voice were all conspiring against him.

What harm would it do to relax and simply savor the moment?

The moment turned into more than two hours, during which they laughed, argued politics and world trade, and enjoyed a simple meal of grilled salmon and a salad of tomatoes and onions marinated in the most amazing dressing Thad had ever tasted.

"I want this recipe," he remarked as he filled his plate a second time.

"You cook?" Heather shot him a look across the patio table.

He shrugged. "When I find the time. Which isn't

often. But there's something satisfying about cooking. Especially over a grill. Ever try it?''

She chuckled. ''Not often. But I do know how to cook. When the spirit moves me, that is.'' She motioned toward his empty mug. ''Want another beer?''

He shook his head. ''No thanks. I have a long drive ahead of me. But if there's coffee, I'd love some.''

Heather walked to the kitchen and returned minutes later with a tray of coffee, cups and saucers, sugar and cream.

While she poured and passed them around, Joe glanced up at the lights of an approaching car. ''Looks like we've got company.''

Minutes later Inez scurried off to the front door and returned, followed by a well-dressed man.

''Graham.'' Joe Colton was on his feet and halfway across the courtyard before his guest could say a word. After greeting him, Joe led him toward the table where Heather and Thad were standing alongside Jackson.

After Heather had greeted her uncle, Joe turned to Thad. ''Detective Thad Law, this is my brother Graham.''

''Detective Law.'' Graham looked from his brother to the detective who towered over him. ''Jackson called me about this latest shooting. I'm sorry I couldn't be here sooner. Business in San Francisco. Have they found the gunman?''

"Not yet. But they're working on it.''

"Yes, this looks like hard work,'' Graham said with a trace of sarcasm.

"Thad's off duty at the moment.'' Joe's usual smile faded a bit. "We were just finishing dinner. Have you eaten?''

"I figured I'd let you feed me.'' Graham, looking dapper in custom-tailored slacks and shirt, settled into a chair and carefully crossed one Italian leather-clad foot over the other. "What were you drinking?'' He looked around and, spotting the empty mugs, gave a laugh. "Beer? I'll have Scotch. Rocks.'' He turned his attention to Thad. "So, Detective, are you close to finding this madman? Or don't you discuss business after hours?''

Thad studied Joe's brother with the same care he used on everyone he met. "Like Joe said, we were just enjoying dinner.''

Joe handed his brother a tumbler of Scotch before settling into the chair beside him. His smile was warm and easy. "Well, Graham, I must say this visit is a pleasant surprise. Jackson thought you wouldn't be here for at least a few more days.''

"A surprise?'' Graham turned to fix him with a look. "You mean Meredith didn't tell you I was coming?''

"She knew?"

Graham nodded. "I called her this morning and told her I was on my way." He glanced around. "Where is Meredith?"

"She had an appointment at LaBelle. She'll be gone for a day or two. That's probably why she forgot to mention your visit. Too much on her mind lately."

Graham visibly relaxed. "Yeah. That's true of all of us." He turned to Thad. "So, Detective, tell us about what you've uncovered so far."

Thad got to his feet. "Sorry. I wish I could. But there's no time." He offered a handshake to Joe. "Thanks for drinks and dinner."

"You're welcome. Let's do it again. Soon."

Thad shook hands with Graham and Jackson.

When he turned to Heather she surprised him by saying, "Come on. I'll see you out."

They left the others in the courtyard as they made their way along a hallway.

"That was very clever of you, Detective."

At Heather's words he paused. "What was?"

"The way you managed to avoid answering any questions."

He laughed. "Part of the job."

They walked to the front door. After opening it, Thad paused on the threshold and turned to her. "I had a great time."

"I'm glad. Does this mean you don't mind that my uncle pressured you into staying?"

Thad shook his head. "Not at all. I'm glad he did. I can't remember the last time I just sat around having a normal discussion with intelligent adults."

Heather laughed. "You make it sound like you spend all your time in the company of babies."

His grin was quick and unexpected. "Something like that." He took a step back, determined not to touch her. "Now I really have to go."

She placed a hand on his arm and felt the heat of his flesh against her palm. "I hope this doesn't mean you have a wife or girlfriend waiting at home for you, Detective."

He absorbed the little jolt to his heart. "Why? Would you mind if I did?"

She laughed again. "If I didn't know better, I'd say you were trying to trap me into revealing something that would be better kept a secret."

"Ah, secrets—my stock in trade. I'm a hardboiled cop, remember?" If she kept her hand there much longer he'd go up in flames. In his best villainous imitation he leaned close and caught her chin in his hand. "Ve have ways of making you talk, woman."

Her laughter faded the moment he touched her. She found herself holding her breath as she whispered, ''The truth? Yes. I'd mind very much. Is there a wife or girlfriend?''

Her honesty was so unexpected, he was momentarily speechless. When he finally found his voice he said, ''No.''

Her breath came out slowly in a sigh of relief.

His own smile was gone, replaced with that heart-stopping look that seemed to wipe every thought from her mind.

For several more seconds Thad waged a terrible battle within himself. He wanted, more than anything, to taste those lips. But he knew he was playing with fire.

Heather saw the way he stared at her mouth and knew, in that instant, that he wanted to kiss her, but was fighting the urge. She leaned forward slightly, inviting him to do the same. When he held back she leaned into him. It seemed the most natural thing in the world to come together in a kiss. But the moment they did, everything changed. The light-hearted banter was forgotten. The voices drifting from the courtyard disappeared.

For Thad, the world seemed to fall away. The only thing he saw was this gilded angel in his arms. The only thing he felt was this need. A hard, driving need that had him taking the kiss deeper and holding on to her as though clinging to life itself.

He breathed in her perfume until it filled his lungs

and had him reeling with need. A need as sharp as any arrow, piercing his heart.

Against her mouth he muttered, "I've been wanting to do this all evening."

"I'm glad. It's what I wanted, too." She wrapped her arms around his neck and gave herself up to the pleasure of his lips.

The kiss went on and on, draining her even as it filled her.

Oh, it felt so good to be held in those strong arms. To be crushed against that muscled chest. To feel these little splinters of fire and ice along her spine. If she could, she would stay just like this all through the night.

"Now I really have to go." He didn't move, didn't release his hold on her.

"I understand." She brushed her lips over his cheek before lifting her head to look into his eyes. "You have...obligations, whatever they are."

He nodded. "I wish I didn't, but I really do have to go." Still, he helped himself to one more bruising kiss that had his heartbeat thundering as though he'd been running up the side of a mountain.

Heather touched a hand to his chest. "Your heart's beating even harder than mine."

"Then I'll just have to see what I can do about that." He dragged her close once more, kissing her so deeply, so thoroughly, her head was spinning. She came up gasping for breath.

He put a hand to her throat and could feel the wild flutter of her pulse. "Uh-huh. That's better."

"Better than what?"

"Better than suffering alone." He found the courage to lower his hands to his sides and take a step back. Then, before he could give in to temptation to touch her again, he turned and walked deliberately to his car.

After he climbed in and switched on the ignition, he turned and looked toward the front door. Heather was still standing there in a circle of light, watching him. She looked like some golden goddess, with the light spilling around her, holding back the darkness.

He lifted a hand in a salute, then drove off.

The taste of her was still on his lips. And the fragrance of crushed roses seemed to be all around him.

Six

Joe Colton looked up from the paperwork on his desk when he saw his wife's car coming up the drive. Without a word to Heather, who was working on the computer, he walked from his office and made his way to the master suite. He was waiting there when she entered.

At the steely look in his eyes Meredith stopped in midstride, seeming to prepare for the full force of his temper. Instead his voice was calm, controlled.

"I spoke with the director at LaBelle."

She brought her hands to her hips. "What right do you have to check up on me?"

"In case you've forgotten, I'm the guy who pays your bills. And this time you've gone too far, Meredith."

Her eyes narrowed to little slits. "What are you talking about?"

"About the amount you charged for this little trip to the spa."

"Are you saying you won't pay it?"

He nodded his head. "Oh, I'll pay it. But it's the last time. I've decided that one of us has to be sensible. And since you can't, I've done what I should have done a long time ago. I've cancelled your credit cards, Meredith. All of them. From now on, when you want anything, you'll have to clear it with me first."

Her voice became the familiar whine. "You can't treat me like this, Joe. I won't stand for it."

He brushed past her and paused in the doorway. "You left me no choice. I can't do much about the way you behave, but I can control my own behavior. I've decided that I'm through playing the fool for you, Meredith. Now if you'll excuse me, I'll leave you alone to admire yourself. Though personally I can't see what you have to show for three days and ten grand spent at the spa."

He closed the door quietly behind him, leaving her alone to brood over this latest event.

Patsy liked Joe Colton better when he was wildly

furious. Then she could push a few of his buttons and send him into a rant, which would cause him no end of remorse. Afterward, he would give her whatever she wanted in order to enjoy a little peace. But this cool, calculating mood was something new and different. She had the distinct impression that he meant to carry out this latest threat.

What would she do without money? She started to pace. She needed a plan. She had to be ready to run if she was found out. She couldn't just uproot two little boys and run from the law without a bankroll.

Oh, if only that ransom money hadn't been marked and she could spend it. What she couldn't do with—

She stopped her pacing as a thought began to form.

There was someone right here at Prosperino with money. Someone who had always been terrified that she'd go to Joe with the truth about their son, Teddy.

She threw back her head and laughed. "Oh, Graham, what a lovely little surprise I have in store for you tonight. You're about to become my very own personal sugar daddy."

She decided to wear her best dress to dinner. First she'd let him look. Maybe she'd even let him touch. But not without paying. And paying dearly.

* * *

Graham sauntered out to the pool and settled onto a lounge beside his son. In the water, Heather was roughhousing with Teddy and Joe, Jr. The two little boys had decided to come at her from either side, hoping to drag her under. Quick as a flash she caught Teddy and tossed him backward, then pinned his older brother's arms to his sides, threatening to do the same to him until he agreed to surrender.

The two boys were having a grand time. Their laughter filled the air as they splashed in the pool, as playful as a pair of young dolphins.

Graham lowered his sunglasses to peer over the top at his son. "That's one beautiful young woman."

"Yeah." Jackson grinned as Heather tossed Teddy again, sending the boy into shrieks of laughter when he surfaced. "She's just so good for those two. I don't know when I've seen them having more fun."

"You could be having fun, too."

Jackson turned to look at his father. "What's that supposed to mean?"

"A pretty young thing like that stuck way out here in the middle of nowhere. I bet she's feeling lonely."

Jackson made a sound of annoyance. "Yeah. She looks lonely, doesn't she?"

The air was filled with more laughter as the two

boys finally managed to push her head under water. She came up sputtering, then, after tossing the hair from her eyes, began swimming after them.

"It's one thing for a woman like that to play with little boys. It's a whole other thing to play with the big boys. If you get my drift. You could do a lot worse than Joe Colton's favorite niece." Graham paused to sip his Scotch, then added, "After all, it isn't as though she's related to you by blood. Why not have yourself a little fun?"

Jackson shrugged. "We get along fine. In fact, better than fine." He watched as she cut cleanly through the water before pulling herself up on the side of the pool and reaching for a towel. "I've always liked Heather."

"There, you see? And she likes you. Don't think I haven't noticed the way she always lights up whenever you're near." Graham leaned back and closed his eyes, content that he'd planted a seed. Now if his son was half the man he thought, this little trip might reap an unexpected bonus.

In Joe Colton's office Detective Thad Law stood at the monitor throwing switches, activating cameras from one end of the ranch to the other. When he activated the camera directed on the pool, he paused, watching the play between Heather and the two little boys.

She looked so natural with them. More like a camp counselor than the smart, savvy, sophisticated woman he'd first met. As she pulled herself out of the water he studied the way she looked with water dripping, her head thrown back in laughter, and felt the quick sexual tug. At almost the same moment he saw Jackson Colton step into camera range and stand beside her, his hand resting lightly on her shoulder.

For the first time in his life Thad felt stirrings of jealousy. It was such an alien feeling he was rocked back on his heels. His first inclination was to deny it. How could he be jealous of someone who wasn't his, could never be his? But there was no denying the flash of unreasonable anger he felt at the sight of Heather and Jackson on the monitor.

He was relieved when Joe Colton entered and started to ask questions about the newest cameras and their positions. Anything was better than standing here watching two beautiful people who obviously belonged together, and wishing it could be otherwise.

Thad had never been a dreamer. There'd been no time for dreams in his demanding life. He was a man driven by a need for order and justice. So why was he punishing himself by wanting something so completely out of his reach?

"I've got news for you, Joe."

Joe Colton paused, his hand on the monitor. "You've got a lead on the gunman?"

Thad shook his head. "No. But the department has put me in charge of this investigation, to the exclusion of all my other duties, except for emergencies."

Seeing the smug look on Joe's face, Thad paused to speculate. "This change in procedure wouldn't be because someone with influence put a little pressure on the department, would it?"

Joe laughed easily. "It might be. But you'll never hear it from my lips." He clapped Thad on the shoulder. "So, it looks like I'll be seeing a whole lot more of you around here."

"Yeah." Thad managed to keep a straight face, but the beginnings of a smile tugged at the corner of his mouth. "You play hardball, don't you, Joe?"

"Damned right." Joe was grinning from ear to ear. "It's one of the perks of having money. I can afford to surround myself with only the best. And I have a feeling that if anybody can solve this mystery, it's you, Thad."

The detective walked away shaking his head. He only hoped Joe's trust hadn't been misplaced.

Right now, every shred of evidence he had seemed to lead directly to Jackson Colton. He had the opportunity. He was at the scene of the crime alone, with no alibi. The only thing he didn't have was a motive. At least not one that Thad could discover. But Thad was a patient man. And maybe now that he'd be able to spend all his time on the case, he'd come up with something conclusive.

"Oh, thanks." Heather wrapped her towel around her hips, saronglike, and accepted a glass of lemonade from Jackson's hand. "Those two wear me out."

"I couldn't figure out who was having more fun. You or the boys."

"It's good to see them having fun. There's been little enough of that in their lives lately."

"Yeah." Jackson nodded. "It can't be easy for them to live with all this tension." He touched a hand to her shoulder. "It can't be easy for you, either."

She shook her head. "I'm fine. But when I heard the sound of that gunshot, I had a few really terrible moments. Not for myself as much as for them." She shuddered. "I didn't know what I'd find upstairs. But whatever it was, I didn't want Teddy and Joe, Jr., to have to see it."

Jackson squeezed her shoulder. "That had to be rough."

"It was." She looked up. Out of the corner of her eye she saw Thad walking toward them.

When he drew close, she could see the tight, angry set of his mouth. His eyes were hidden behind mirrored sunglasses.

"Something wrong, Detective?" Jackson turned toward Thad, keeping his hand on Heather's shoulder.

"Nothing." Thad looked at Heather. "I just wanted to inform you that the department has assigned me to your uncle's case on a full-time basis until it's solved."

"Oh, Thad. Uncle Joe will be so relieved."

"I just gave him the news."

They were interrupted by shouts from Teddy and Joe, Jr., who were clearly unhappy at having Heather's time monopolized by the men.

"Oh. You want more, do you?" With a laugh she handed her glass to Jackson and untied her towel, flinging it on a chaise. Then in a most unladylike manner she dove into the pool and began swimming, to the delighted squeals of two little boys.

"She's incredible, isn't she?" Jackson turned to watch the chase.

"Yeah. Incredible." Thad was grateful for the sunglasses. He was able to watch her without fear of revealing what was going through his mind.

Patsy stood in front of the full-length mirror studying her reflection. She'd tried on four dresses before settling on this one. It was revealing enough to pique Graham's interest, and modest enough to keep Joe from snarling. She liked the way the fabric hugged her body in the most suggestive way. And the honey tones played up her eyes. She slid her feet into honey-colored sandals with sexy stiletto heels before making her way to the dining room.

Joe and the boys were already there, along with Heather and Jackson. She barely gave them a nod before pouring herself a drink. But when Graham walked in, she saw the way he looked her over and her mood lifted considerably. She realized she was actually looking forward to tonight. There was nothing quite as satisfying as sparring with a man who was as transparent as glass.

She ate mechanically, allowing the others to carry the conversation throughout the tedious meal. She had a vague sense that Jackson was making a move on Heather, but she was too preoccupied to pay much attention. Besides, she could see by the look in Heather's eyes that she wasn't feeling anything toward the young man seated beside her. A woman always knew those things. There was no spark between them, no sizzle.

Now the detective was another story. There was something going on between him and Heather. Patsy hadn't yet figured out if he was annoyed or attracted. She tried to keep as much distance as possible between herself and Thaddeus Law. He made her far too uncomfortable.

She was relieved when dinner was finally over, and even more relieved when Joe offered to go upstairs and read to the boys. Heather and Jackson drifted out to the courtyard, leaving Patsy alone with Graham.

She pushed away from the table and crossed to a sideboard. "Want another Scotch?"

"Sure. You having one?"

She nodded and filled two tumblers. When she handed one to him, she turned in such a way that his arm grazed her breast. She saw his eyes narrow a fraction and knew that he'd felt it. Oh, he was so easy.

"We need to talk, Graham."

He huffed out a laugh. "Are you sure that's what you have in mind?"

"Yeah. Very sure. Once with you was enough."

His smile faded. "You said we'd never mention that."

"Did I?" She gave him a sly smile. "Maybe I lied."

"What?" He set down his drink with a clatter.

Her smile grew. "I wonder what would happen to you if Joe found out our little secret."

His face contorted into anger. "You wouldn't dare."

"Oh, wouldn't I?" She stepped closer and ran one perfectly manicured fingernail down the front of his shirt. "Of course, there's a way to ensure my silence."

"How? Slit your throat?"

She merely smiled. "You don't have the nerve for that, Graham, and you know it. But there's a much easier way to guarantee that it always remains our little secret."

He glared at her. "I'm waiting."

"Money. Three million dollars, to be exact."

Graham swallowed back the rage that threatened to choke him. Fighting to keep his tone even, he said, "Three million is just a bit rich for my blood."

"Really?" She looked him up and down. "That's pretty hard to believe coming from a man wearing a twenty-thousand-dollar watch, three-hundred-dollar loafers, and four-hundred-dollar custom-tailored slacks."

Graham flushed. She was a lot more observant than he'd thought. Still, the fact that the gunman was on the loose was a hopeful sign. Joe could find himself in an assassin's sight at any time. And when it happened, as Joe's only brother, he stood to inherit a fortune. Three million would be pocket change.

"Look, Meredith." He kept his tone easy, his touch gentle as he tilted up her face, forcing her to look into his eyes. "I feel a sense of responsibility about you and Teddy. And I've always prided myself on being a man who takes care of his own. If you'll agree to two million, I can manage it, as long as you let me pay you a little at a time.''

Her eyes glittered with greed. "How little?"

He felt a thrill of victory and struggled not to gloat. "How about a hundred thousand now, and the rest later?''

She pretended to consider. In fact, it was more than she'd hoped for. After a moment she nodded. "All right. I want it in cash."

"Of course. You don't think I want to leave a trail of checks, do you?"

Patsy patted his cheek. "That's what I've always loved about you, Graham. You and I are on the same wavelength.'' She pressed herself closer. "Want to seal the bargain?''

He glanced toward the door, relieved to hear the sound of someone coming. "You know I'd love to, but not here in Joe's house."

"It's my house, too."

"Yes, of course." He stepped back and actually smiled when the housekeeper entered. "I'll have that package delivered inside of a couple of weeks.''

As he beat a hasty retreat to the door, Patsy called after him, "Make it sooner."

"A week, then." He drained his Scotch in one long swallow and went off in search of friendlier company.

Seven

"You're leaving?" Joe was enjoying morning coffee in the courtyard when his brother entered at the same moment that he spotted Jackson carrying luggage to his car.

Graham helped himself to a cup and struggled to paste on a thin smile. After his encounter last night with Meredith, he couldn't wait to escape. "We've enjoyed your hospitality long enough. Besides, I really just wanted to see for myself that you were all right after this latest incident. Now that I know you're in the capable hands of Detective Law, I think it's time to get back to work."

He saw his son stop to chat with Heather and nodded toward the two young people. "They make a handsome couple, don't you think?"

Joe shrugged. "I doubt that it matters what you or I think. It's what they think that counts." He arched a brow. "Is Jackson interested in Heather?"

Graham frowned. "Who knows with kids today. He hasn't said one way or the other."

"I wouldn't worry." Joe drained his cup. "They'll have plenty of opportunities to get together. If they're meant to be, it'll happen in its own sweet time."

"Thanks for that bit of wisdom." Graham stuck out his hand. "Time to go. We've got a long drive ahead of us." He set aside his coffee, eager to be on his way.

"I'll walk with you to the car." Joe and his brother made their way to where Jackson and Heather were waiting.

After handshakes all around, and hugs between Jackson and Heather, Graham and his son settled themselves into separate cars. Minutes later Joe and Heather stood watching as they sped along the drive.

Joe glanced at his watch. "I'm going to be spending most of the afternoon in conference calls. Let's see if we can clear the last of the paperwork off my desk in the next hour or so." He sighed. "Thanks to you, we've managed to work our way through the bulk of it these past weeks.''

''I told you.'' Heather kept pace beside him. ''We make a great team.''

He grinned. ''That we do, sweetheart. But for the next couple of days there won't be much work for the team.''

''Why?''

''Because one member is going to be spending an awful lot of time on the phone.''

''Then I'll just have to find something to occupy my time.''

Joe held his office door for her, then followed her inside. ''There's always Diablo.''

Heather gave him an impish grin. ''That's exactly what I was thinking.''

Heather waved to Joe as she walked out of his office. From the tone of his conversation, he would be tied up for the next hour or more with executives from Colton Enterprises.

She wandered to the kitchen and helped herself to iced tea before heading out the door. As she walked into the fresh air she breathed deeply and tipped back her head to take a long swallow. With a sigh of contentment she set the tall glass on the porch railing. As she did, she caught sight of a little girl dancing through the garden, chasing after a butterfly.

A little girl?

Heather glanced around for the child's mother. Seeing no one nearby, she walked closer and dropped to her knees in front of the child.

"Hello. Aren't you beautiful!"

And she was. With long raven ringlets that fell to her shoulders and big eyes the color of cobalt. Added to that were the sweetest dimples when she smiled, making her absolutely stunning.

She was dressed in an adorable little dress of ice-blue. On her feet were canvas sneakers.

"What's your name?"

"Brittany," the little girl said softly.

"Brittany. Oh, that suits you. It's as beautiful as you are."

Again that smile that could melt glaciers.

"Where's your mama and daddy, Brittany?"

The little girl shrugged, then pointed at the butterfly, flitting from branch to branch of a nearby tree. "Oh, look. Isn't it pretty?"

"Yes, it is." Heather picked up the little girl so that she could reach the branches. "See?"

The butterfly swooped, almost touching the outstretched hand, before flying away.

"Is it gone?" Brittany asked.

"Yes. I'm afraid it's gone. But maybe we'll find

another.'' Heather set the child on her feet and caught her little hand in hers, leading her toward the house. ''Are you hungry?''

Brittany nodded.

''All right.'' At the porch Heather lifted her in her arms and carried her into the kitchen, setting her on a chair at the table. ''You sit here and I'll try to figure out what you can eat. But first, we'd better tie a bib over that pretty little outfit.''

Taking a tea towel from a kitchen drawer, Heather fashioned a bib.

It didn't take too much effort to learn that little Brittany liked almost anything. Heather fixed a plate containing cereal in the shape of letters, pieces of cheese, and slices of red, ripe strawberries. Between bites, the child was happy to sip from a glass of apple juice.

They looked up as the door was yanked open and Thad Law stood scowling at the two of them.

''Daddy,'' the little girl chirped.

''Daddy?'' Heather knew her mouth was open, but she couldn't seem to close it. ''She's...yours?''

For a moment Thad was beyond words. He simply scooped up the little girl and hugged her fiercely, closing his eyes as his ragged breathing subsided and the pounding of his heart gradually slowed.

But as his fear drained away, a newer, stronger emotion replaced it. A dark, blinding fury.

Very carefully he set down his daughter before lashing out at Heather. "What gives you the right to touch her? How dare you take her out of my car without my permission?"

"Your car?" She stared at him, trying to keep up with his shift in moods. "Are you saying you left this little girl in your car?"

"Don't play coy with me. Just answer the question."

"And just what is your question, Detective Law?"

Surprise overcame anger. He gaped at her, then tried again. "Wait a minute. You didn't take her from my car?"

"I found her wandering around in the garden. So I brought her in and fixed her something to eat." She glanced at the child who was now happily eating the rest of her strawberries.

Thad did the same and could see that she'd been carefully tended.

"Are you telling me Brittany got out of my car by herself?"

"If she didn't, there must be a genie nearby." Now it was Heather's turn to lose her temper. "I can't believe anybody with even half a brain would leave a child alone in a car. Especially a man trained in safety. What did you expect her to do all day?"

"I didn't intend to be here all day. More like half

an hour. I wouldn't have come at all except that there was a report that one of the silent alarms went off at headquarters.''

"But why would you bring a baby along?''

"I'm not a baby,'' the little girl called.

Both Heather and Thad glanced down to see her looking up at them.

"I'm a big girl, Daddy. You said so.''

"Yes, you are, honey.'' He lifted her up and pressed a kiss to her hand. "Would you show Daddy how you got out of his car?''

"Okay.'' She was laughing up into his eyes as he turned away.

Heather started after him. "This I've got to see.''

When they reached his car he opened the back door and set Brittany in her child seat, handing her a teddy bear before fastening the seat belt.

"That's all she had to occupy her time?''

He gave Heather a withering look. "I told you. I expected to be no more than half an hour.''

"To a child, that could seem like eternity.''

Her remark went right to his heart, since he knew it was the truth. To spare himself he decided to ignore it.

He turned back to his daughter. "Show Daddy what you did, honey.''

Brittany's little lips turned into a pout. "Teddy fell down.'' She dropped the bear to the floor. "So

I had to get him.'' She pressed the release on her seat belt, then climbed down and picked up the bear, setting it in her seat. ''Teddy said he wanted to take a nap, so I let him.'' With her fingers to her lips, to indicate that she would be quiet, she climbed into the front seat and jiggled the buttons on the door until the locks clicked. Then she opened the door.

''See, Daddy?'' She was so proud of her accomplishment, he had no choice but to pick her up and kiss her little mouth.

Over her head he said to Heather, ''I'm really sorry about that scene back there. I was scared out of my mind when I found my car empty. I was terrified that someone had snatched her.''

''Apology accepted. I don't blame you for being half-mad with fear. I would be, too.'' She paused. ''Why did you bring her with you?''

''Because the neighbor who usually sits for her had to fly out to be with her daughter, who's about to have a baby. And the girl who was supposed to replace her didn't show. I had no option.''

''Where's Brittany's mother?''

''She's dead.''

It was the last thing Heather had expected to hear. For the space of a moment she was too stunned to speak. Then she touched a hand to his arm. ''Oh, Thad. I'm sorry.''

"It was three years ago. Brittany was only a year old. She doesn't even remember her mother."

"And you've been taking care of Brittany alone?"

"Yeah." He turned toward the car. "Thanks for rescuing her. But I think we'd better go home now."

Heather surprised even herself by saying, "If you have something more to do here, I could take care of her."

"You?" He turned back, staring at her as though she'd just announced she was an ax murderer.

She looked slightly embarrassed. "I don't know much about very young children. But we seemed to be getting along just fine before you came storming in."

"What about your own work?"

She shrugged. "Uncle Joe said we were through for the day. And since I have nothing else planned..." Her voice trailed off.

He was studying her so closely she felt the heat rise to her cheeks.

"You're serious, aren't you?"

"Of course I am."

He considered for a moment longer. Then he said to Brittany, "Would you like to stay with Heather for a while, honey?"

The little girl clapped her hands in delight, then held out her arms.

For a moment it was a toss-up as to which of them was more shocked—Thad or Heather.

Thad reluctantly handed her over to Heather and the little girl wrapped her chubby arms around her neck. "Can I have more berries?"

"If your daddy says so." Heather glanced over at him.

It took Thad a minute to compose himself. It gave him the oddest feeling to see his daughter in the arms of this woman.

When he didn't answer, Heather said, "Thad, is it okay?"

He blinked. "Is what okay?"

"If Brittany has more strawberries?"

"Yeah, sure."

"Good." She arched a brow. "Is something wrong?"

He shook his head. "No. Nothing's wrong. And, Heather?"

She turned to look at him, and he was struck by the two pair of eyes watching him. One pair soft sky-blue, the other same midnight-blue as his own.

"Thanks. I really appreciate this."

She laughed. "Maybe you'd better not thank me yet. You'd be wise to wait and see if I'm up to the task."

* * *

It was after five o'clock when Thad finally wrote up his report and headed toward the house. Along the way he stopped at his car and tossed his suit jacket and tie into the back seat. Then, rolling the sleeves of his white shirt, he crossed the yard and paused at the kitchen.

Inez directed him to the courtyard, where he found Heather seated in a rocker with Brittany on her lap. Both were asleep. The little girl's head was resting in the crook of Heather's bent arm. A children's storybook had dropped to the floor at their feet. On a table beside them was a sweating glass of lemonade. Since all the ice had melted, Thad decided they'd both been sleeping for some time.

He knelt in front of them, feeling such a welling of love and peace in his heart. A far cry from what he'd felt when he'd first discovered his daughter missing from his car. He'd never known such icy terror in all his life.

He supposed it went with the territory. As a police detective, he was forced to deal with the dregs of humanity. He knew, more than most, just what unspeakable things man could do to man.

But as a father, he would do anything, pay any price, even at the cost of his own life, to spare his child even the smallest pain. There had been a few moments when he'd been almost blind with fear.

The relief he'd felt when he saw his daughter calmly eating had been the most overwhelming feeling he'd ever experienced.

He studied the woman holding his daughter in the circle of her arms. Her head was bent to one side, her lips pressed to Brittany's forehead. A diamond and emerald tennis bracelet winking at her wrist was almost hidden by Brittany's long black curls. The slacks she was wearing had probably cost what he earned in a day. Yet she seemed oblivious to the fact that they would be sweaty and wrinkled when she relinquished her hold on his little girl. The same was true of her silk blouse. It bore the evidence of berry stains and tiny hand smudges. Yet, if the smile on her face was any indication, she didn't seem to mind in the least.

As he watched the way the woman and child were breathing in a slow, steady rhythm, he felt the strangest ache around his heart.

At that moment Heather awoke. For the space of a single moment she looked confused. Then she glanced over at the little girl in her arms and smiled at him.

"I was reading her a story."

"Yeah." Needing something to do, he pretended that he'd been retrieving the book. He looked at the cover. "Goldilocks and the Three Bears?"

Heather chuckled. "It was the only one I could

find in Teddy's room that was suitable for a little girl.''

At the sound of their voices Brittany stretched and yawned, then reached out her arms toward her father.

He picked her up and hugged her to his chest. ''Did you have fun with Heather?''

''Uh-huh.'' She hugged him back, then said, ''She was reading me a story, Daddy. It was called Ravenlocks and the Three Bears.''

He glanced over her head to Heather. ''Ravenlocks?''

Brittany answered. ''Uh-huh. And she said the bears are cousins of my teddy bear. They're really nice bears, Daddy. And tonight I'm going to leave some honey on the table for them, in case they want to visit our house.''

Thad couldn't keep the laughter from his voice. ''You're leaving honey out for the bears? Are you sure you want them to visit?''

''Only if they're polite. Heather said polite bears always say please and thank you.''

''Heather is absolutely right.'' He stepped back as Heather got to her feet. ''Well, since Brittany and I don't want to be outdone by the bears, we'd like to say thank you, too.'' He held out his hand. ''I really appreciate this, Heather.''

She accepted his handshake and absorbed the jolt

to her system. There was no denying that his touch always had this effect on her.

As he started across the courtyard she called, "What will you do with Brittany tomorrow?"

He shrugged. "I'll start making some phone calls as soon as I get home. There are several day-care centers in town."

"I...wouldn't mind taking her for the next couple of days."

He shot her a look of surprise. "What about your work?"

"Uncle Joe said there wouldn't be much for me to do for the next couple of days."

"Yeah. Well, I'm sure you'd rather be riding or shopping or..."

She was already shaking her head. "Really, Thad. We had such a good time together. I never realized just how much fun it could be. Why not let her come with you and let me take care of her? That way you can see her often during the day and decide whether or not I'm doing a good job. Isn't that better than leaving her with strangers?"

"You're serious, aren't you?" He studied her for the longest time before nodding his head. "Okay. Let's give it a try. But if you decide you've had enough, I'll expect you to be honest with me." He held out his hand. "Is it a deal?"

"Deal." This time she was ready for the jolt.

As he walked away she realized she was still vibrating from his touch. And wishing for more.

She ran across the courtyard and called, "Bye, Brittany. See you tomorrow." Under her breath she added, "And your big bad doting daddy, too."

Eight

"**I**'m not happy with these sensors. They're not picking up the right signals. Let's try moving them to the right." Thad motioned to a workman standing on a ladder, then turned with a look of annoyance at the interruption.

When he caught sight of Brittany being towed in a wagon by Heather, his frown turned into a wide smile.

The little girl climbed out and raced toward her father, who scooped her up in his arms and was rewarded with wet kisses.

"Umm." He kissed her cheeks. "Now that's the

nicest thing that's happened to me all day. What are you and Heather doing in the stable?''

"Heather said I could pet a horse.'' She looked up at him. "Have you ever petted a horse, Daddy?''

"Not in a very long time.''

"Then you have to come with us. Hurry, Daddy, put me down. I don't want the horse to think I'm a baby.''

Thad grinned as he set her on her feet.

"Come on, Daddy.'' She caught his hand.

He glanced over her head at Heather, who joined them. "I hope we're not heading toward Diablo's stall.''

"I told you I was reckless, not foolish.'' With a laugh she led them to a stall and opened the door to lead them inside. "Brittany, this is Lucy.''

"Why did you name her Lucy?'' the little girl asked, holding back at the sight of the big creature.

"Because she's a redhead.''

Heather and Thad exchanged grins as they realized that the joke was lost on someone so young.

Heather lifted Brittany up and brought her closer to the mare. It stood perfectly still, as though sensing the little girl's fear.

"Ooh. She's soft.'' Brittany laughed with delight when her fingers came in contact with the soft muzzle. "Feel, Daddy.''

Thad obligingly placed his hand alongside that of his daughter. "Yeah. She sure is soft, honey."

Her fears forgotten, Brittany asked, "Can I sit on her back, Heather?"

"I'll leave that up to your father."

Seeing his concern, Heather said in an aside, "Lucy's as gentle as they come. All she'll do is stand there. I give you my word."

He nodded. "Okay, honey. Here goes." He took her from Heather and placed her on the mare's back.

As promised, the old horse stood perfectly still.

Brittany was enchanted. "When I get big can I ride her?"

"Would you like that?" Thad asked.

"Uh-huh." Brittany's eyes were wide with excitement. "Heather said she rides horses. And when I get big, I want to ride them, too."

Thad lifted her into his arms and pressed his lips to her cheek. "I hope you're going to wait a few years for that."

"For what, Daddy?"

"For getting bigger."

Brittany looked at him in surprise. "Why?"

"Because I really like having you just the way you are." He handed her over to Heather. "Thanks for letting me pet the horse. But now I'd better get back to work."

As the two walked back to the wagon Thad heard

his daughter saying solemnly, "When I grow up, I'm going to be a policeman just like Daddy."

Heather's reply was carried on the breeze. "That's a fine thing to be. What would we do without policemen to keep us safe?"

"But I want to ride horses like you, too," the little girl added.

"Maybe you could be a mounted policeman. Then you'd get to ride horses all day while you work."

Thad turned and watched as Heather pulled the wagon across the meadow toward the big house. She always seemed to know just the right thing to say to his daughter. None of the million and one questions typically asked in a day seemed foolish or trivial. And she spent so much time with Brittany. Time to listen. Time to talk. And like this little visit to the stable, time to indulge her slightest whim, or satisfy her every curiosity.

He'd never seen his daughter as happy as she'd been these past few days. Maybe that was why his heart was feeling so much lighter lately.

He frowned. Of course that was the reason. He much preferred believing that to the alternative— that his happiness was in direct proportion to the amount of time he was spending in the company of his daughter's pretty baby-sitter.

* * *

It had been a particularly frustrating day for Thad. He'd been called to the station early, which meant waking his little daughter from a sound sleep and dressing her while she was barely awake. By the time they'd arrived at the ranch, he was grateful to turn his daughter over to the care of Heather, who managed, with a few simple words, to soothe the little girl's unhappiness while calmly fixing a breakfast of fruit, cereal and juice. By the time Thad had seen Brittany at lunchtime, she'd been laughing and chatting as though she hadn't a care in the world.

That went a long way toward making the rest of the day tolerable. But it couldn't ease Thad's uneasiness over the lax security around the ranch. Despite the security monitors and the trained professionals who'd been hired to see to the safety of those who lived here, he had some real reservations about the effectiveness of men and equipment.

Men, even those well paid, tended to get careless. And machines were often affected by weather conditions, or even something as simple as a weak battery.

He frowned as he went over a mental checklist of things he still wanted to look over. He had a friend who had left the police force in San Francisco to form his own private security business. Thad intended to phone him with a list of questions. It never hurt to pick the brains of the best in the business.

Preoccupied, he was walking some distance from the pool when he saw the tiny head bobbing in the water. For one brief moment his heart simply stopped beating. Then he flew into action, racing to the edge, prepared to dive in. Just then he caught sight of Heather standing a foot away from Brittany, urging her to paddle toward her.

When a shadow fell over them she looked up to see Thad scowling at her.

Brittany called, "Look, Daddy. I'm swimming." She splashed through the water until she reached the safety of Heather's arms, where she was caught and held firmly.

Thad's tone was vibrating with a fear so palpable, it had him by the throat. He swallowed it back, preferring to deal in anger. "You're teaching my daughter to swim without checking with me?"

"Sorry." Heather brushed water from her eyes. "You weren't around to ask. And since this was an emergency, I thought I'd better see to it right away. Especially when I realized that she has no fear of water."

Thad's scowl deepened. "What are you talking about?"

"Brittany and I were walking and she ran ahead, right up to the edge of the pool." She touched a hand to her heart. "Thad, she didn't even slow down. She just took a tumble right in."

She kept her arms around the laughing, splashing little girl as she added, "If you think you were afraid the day she was missing from your car, you have some idea how my heart was pounding when I jumped in after her."

She glanced down at the little girl in her arms. "Come on, honey. That's enough for today."

She waded through the water to the edge and handed Brittany up to her father. It was then that he realized the little girl was wearing only her underwear.

"Her clothes are in the dryer along with mine," Heather explained when she caught the look of surprise on his face.

She pulled herself up to the side of the pool and Thad couldn't help but note the tank suit that fit her like a second skin. His anger took a definite second place to a newer emotion.

He reached down and helped her to her feet, his hands lingering on hers a moment longer than necessary before he turned away and handed her a towel.

"Thanks." She dried herself and draped the towel around her shoulders while she found a second towel for Brittany. Soon the little girl was bundled snugly and carried in her father's arms toward the house, with Heather walking beside them.

"I know you're not happy about this, Thad. But

I think you'll agree that it was in Brittany's best interest to teach her water safety as quickly as possible. I decided it was necessary for Brittany to know how to save her own life by rolling to her back and floating until someone manages to haul her out of the water.''

He couldn't hide his skepticism. ''You really think you can teach a four-year-old such a thing?''

She nodded. ''When I was in college I worked at a children's camp. That was the first thing everyone had to learn. No matter how young. We even taught mothers with infants all about water safety.''

When they stepped into the house she left him in the kitchen and returned with Brittany's clothes, which were now dry. He watched as she smoothly dressed the little girl before handing her a snack of fruit and a cup of juice.

''What camp did you work at?'' He couldn't tear his gaze from her as she slipped into a terry robe, cinching the waist.

He'd heard of several exclusive camps in California costing thousands of dollars a week for the children of the rich and privileged. He could imagine Heather in such a place. She'd fit right in.

''It's a camp for families from the inner city who never get to swim in an Olympic-sized pool, or ride a horse, or walk a country road.''

"You worked as a counselor at a camp for the underprivileged?"

"Yeah." She smiled, remembering. "I really loved it. Those are some of my happiest memories. You should see how those families open up to one another when they're taken out of their usual environment and have a chance to just relax and play together."

She turned away and stepped into canvas slippers, completely missing the stunned look on his face.

She was, he realized, a constant surprise. Every day he learned something new about her. But so much of it didn't add up. She was, in fact, becoming more of a puzzle all the time.

A beautiful, beguiling puzzle that he wanted to put together, piece by enticing piece, until he knew her as well as he knew himself.

Thad was feeling hot, sweaty, tired and frustrated. He'd been testing a theory, running from a spot beneath Joe Colton's window to the stable, across the hill to the high meadow and out to the highway.

He checked his stopwatch and swore. Judging by the time the police first logged their arrival on the scene after that second shot was fired, this couldn't have been the escape route of the gunman. Not unless he was an Olympic runner.

Thad was in top physical condition. It would take

a man of extraordinary speed to beat him. Which meant that his entire theory had just gone up in smoke. As had half a dozen earlier ones.

Where had the gunman come from? Where had he gone? And most important of all, when would he strike again?

Thad had no illusions that a man who had made two attempts on Joe Colton's life would simply give up. Whatever drove a man to attempt to take another man's life wouldn't be easily forgotten. Whether the motive was money or revenge, neither would be satisfied until the deed was accomplished.

Which led him back to Jackson Colton.

What if the gunman had no intention of running? What if he'd planned to let himself inside, mingle with the family, and make certain that this time the job was finished to his satisfaction?

He hated the fact that every road led him back to the same suspect. Especially since Joe Colton seemed to have real affection for his nephew. But affection or no, Thad had a job to do. And he intended to see it through to the end, no matter where that end might be.

He trudged back to the house in search of his daughter and was directed to Joe's office. Inside he found Joe down on his hands and knees beside Heather, who was watching Brittany. All three were laughing as Joe dipped a wand into a jar of bubbles and blew, causing the little girl to reach out wildly trying to catch them.

Each time another bubble disappeared she would call out, "Look. They're all gone."

Heather and Joe, like parrots, would repeat the phrase and then roar with laughter.

"Thad." Joe looked up with a smile that spread from ear to ear. "I'd forgotten how much fun little people can be. Watch this." He dipped the wand and blew, causing squeals of delight from Brittany as she burst each bubble.

Thad felt all the weariness slowly dissolve. He stood for long minutes watching as his daughter began to chase an errant bubble that floated, drifted, tumbled on a draught of air.

"Look, Daddy." She caught the bubble, and giggled hysterically when it burst. Then she raced over to him and lifted her arms. "Kisses?"

"Oh, yes. Lots and lots of kisses." He sighed as her chubby arms wrapped around his neck and her wet lips were pressed to his cheek. This was all he ever needed to feel completely restored. The heat and frustration of the day were forgotten.

He turned to Heather. "I can't thank you enough. You'll never know how great it's been knowing my daughter was close by, and having so much love and attention showered on her."

"She's a wonderful little girl, Thad. And it's obvious she's been treated with a lot of love in her young life.''

"Yeah. Well, loving her is easy.'' He shifted Brittany to his other arm and stuck out his hand. "Thanks for all you've done. I'll spend the weekend finding something more permanent.''

She accepted his handshake, fighting to ignore the heat she knew would follow his touch. "You don't have to, Thad. I love taking care of Brittany.''

He shook his head, determined to do this. He'd been giving it a great deal of thought. He simply couldn't impose on Heather and Joe any longer. Besides, he was beginning to feel a little too...comfortable with this arrangement. It was time to sever this connection before it got even more comfortable.

"You two have work to do. And it won't get done if you're spending all your time baby-sitting.'' He turned to the little girl in his arms. "Can you say thank-you to Heather and Uncle Joe for the grand week you've spent with them?''

She dimpled. "Thank you, Heather. Thank you, Uncle Joe.'' Then she surprised them by holding out her arms to Heather. "Kisses,'' she demanded.

Heather took her from Thad and was immediately covered with baby kisses. She gathered the little girl close, breathing her in, and found herself wondering how she'd lived for so long without something this special in her life.

She never would have believed that something as simple as caring for the needs of a little girl could transform her life so completely. She'd never felt so satisfied as she had this week. How could corporate work compare with the challenge of keeping up with one tiny whirlwind?

When Thad tried to take her back, Brittany's little arms tightened around Heather's neck. "No, Daddy. I want Heather to carry me to the car."

Heather laughed. "I bribed her to say that. Next I'm going to teach her to say she loves me best."

Thad gave a rumble of laughter. "A word of warning. My patience only stretches so thin. I can tolerate a lot of things, but not that. If I'm not number one in my daughter's life, I may have to make the life of a certain party awfully miserable until she backs off. Understood?"

"Oh yes. I hear you loud and clear, Detective." Still laughing, Heather led the way, with Thad following.

Joe crossed his arms over his chest and leaned a hip against his desk, considering. If he didn't know better, he'd say there was some kind of chemistry between his niece and this hard-boiled detective. Not that he'd mind. He thought the world of both of them. Still, he was pretty sure Heather's father and mother had other plans for her. Not to mention his brother, Graham, who was hoping for a match between Heather and his son, Jackson.

Joe watched through the window as the couple stood by Thad's car, the little girl between them. Even from this distance, their body language spoke volumes as Heather handed Brittany over to Thad.

Joe wondered if either of them was listening to what their bodies were saying.

Not that it mattered. They'd hear the whispers in time. Whispers that would grow louder with every passing day.

Suddenly he threw back his head and roared with laughter. Wait until they discovered that love had a way of sneaking up on a couple when they least expected it.

He'd pay a fortune to see the looks on their faces when the knowledge finally dawned.

Nine

Heather was in her room, lost in her favorite futuristic detective novel, when her cell phone rang.

The sound of Thad's voice caught her by surprise. "Thad, what's wrong?"

"I'm sorry to bother you so late, but I didn't have anyone else to turn to. My neighbors all seem to be out. Nobody's answering their phones. I have this whole network of friends I can turn to in an emergency, but I can't find any of them just now when I need them."

"What is it, Thad?" Her heart did a little flip. "Is it Brittany?"

"Yeah. A fever. I just talked to her pediatrician, and I need to run out for some medicine. The only trouble is, I can't leave her alone, and I hate to take her out when she's so sick."

"I'll be right there. Just give me directions."

She listened carefully, writing down the directions to his place, before disconnecting and grabbing up her purse. Downstairs she went in search of her uncle and found him still at his desk.

"Thad just called. He needs me to stay with Brittany while he picks up some medicine."

Joe reached into his pocket and tossed her a set of keys. "Take the Land Rover. It's parked in the drive."

"Thanks, Uncle Joe. I appreciate this."

He waved aside her words. "We have more than enough cars around this ranch. But be sure and take your phone with you, sweetheart."

She held it up. "I have it. I don't know when I'll be back."

"Don't worry about a thing. Just take care of that sweet little girl."

She brushed a kiss over his cheek and hurried out the door.

Joe glanced at the clock on his desk. Almost midnight on a Friday night.

If he were a betting man, he'd take odds that this weekend could mark the beginning of a whole new chapter in the life of his niece and Detective Thad Law.

After all, fireworks of any kind were best experienced after dark.

If the fireworks that had been building between these two were dazzling enough, he wouldn't be surprised if he didn't see her again until Monday.

Thad was standing in the doorway of his apartment when Heather hurried up the walk. In his arms was his little daughter, holding tightly to him.

His face was tight with worry. His voice a growl of frustration. "What took you so long?"

She didn't bother to tell him she'd broken every speed limit between here and the ranch. And now that she knew him better, she understood that his bark was worse than his bite. Besides, he wasn't angry. He was scared. Like any father would be. She touched a hand to the little girl's forehead and could feel the heat radiating from her.

"Have you sponged her?"

"The doctor didn't say anything about sponging her. He just told me to pick up a fever reducer."

"All right." She held out her arms. "Why don't you see to that, and I'll sponge her with cool water." As she took the child from him she asked, "Where's her room? She needs to be in her bed."

"Right through that hallway."

He was already out the door before Heather had time to drop her purse on a nearby table.

"All right now, honey." Heather carried the weeping child to her bed and realized that the pillowcase was damp with sweat and tears. Working quickly she changed the bedding. "You lie here and I'm going to make you feel cooler."

By the time Thad returned, Brittany was lying on clean sheets, a cool cloth on her forehead. Heather had dimmed the lights, and a tape of children's lullabies played softly in the background.

Heather had positioned a chair beside the bed, so that she could hold the little girl's hand in hers. She was a sea of calm in a scene that had been, just an hour earlier, frantic chaos.

Thad removed a bottle of red liquid from a bag and read the directions before holding the measuring dropper to Brittany's lips. She swallowed, then surprised him by saying, "That tastes good, Daddy. Is it soda?"

When he nodded, Heather gently corrected him by saying, "What your daddy meant to say is that it's medicine, honey. And you can only take it when your father gives his permission. Do you understand?"

"Is that right, Daddy? Is it medicine?"

Thad realized his mistake instantly, and felt a wave of gratitude for this young woman's quick thinking. By suggesting that good-tasting medicine was something as harmless as soda, he could have invited disaster.

"Heather is right, honey. This is medicine to make you feel better. You should never taste it unless I say so."

"Okay." In the little girl's mind, the incident was already forgotten. "Heather was telling me a story, Daddy. Do you want to hear it?"

He sighed, feeling utterly exhausted. After putting in a full day at the ranch, and then finding Brittany burning with an unexplained fever, and having no one nearby to call on, his nerves had taken a tremendous beating. "Yeah. I'd like that."

"Then you have to lie here beside me and be real quiet, Daddy." She patted the bed.

With a grin he eased off his shoes and stretched out beside his daughter, gathering her close.

Heather glanced at the little girl. "Do you want me to start over, or just tell you the end?"

"You have to start all over, so Daddy knows the story, too."

"Okay." Heather felt a warm glow at the way the child snuggled against her father's big chest. "Like all good stories, it has to begin with Once Upon A Time."

Brittany's voice took up the story. "There was a beautiful princess named Brittany, who lived in the magical kingdom of California. And she had a horse that could fly and a puppy that could talk. In people language." Hearing her father's chuckle she turned her head. "Do you already know this story, Daddy?"

"No. I don't believe I do."

"Then you can't laugh, Daddy. You have to listen."

He studied Heather as she sat beside the bed. She was wearing some sort of gauzy midriff blouse that clung to her curves in the most delicious way. And narrow drawstring pants in the same gauzy material. Between the top and pants was an enticing strip of naked skin. It was, he realized, just enough to make a man drool.

Or make him crazy.

To keep from staring at forbidden fruit he closed his eyes and pressed his lips to his little girl's cheek. And listened as Heather's voice washed over him. He'd never felt so relieved, or so relaxed. With his daughter no longer crying, and his fears beginning to dissolve, he let himself drift on a cloud of contentment, while that velvet voice continued to soothe and lull.

It was the last coherent thought he had before he slept.

Heather watched as father and daughter slept side by side. They were such a contrast. This great bear of a man and the tiny, delicate China doll. But there was no denying that Brittany was her father's daughter. The same raven hair, and those soulful eyes, like deep pools that could, with a single look, pull her in.

They'd both managed to wrap themselves around her heart. And now Heather was bound, as firmly as though she'd been chained to them.

She hadn't meant for this to happen. In fact, it was the last thing she'd wanted. She'd come here to Prosperino seeking freedom. And a man with a four-year-old child would hardly equal that. Especially one as tough and demanding as Thad Law. But there it was. She'd lost her heart to both of them. It was hard now to remember which one had come first. Had it been Thad, with that tough-guy attitude and that take-charge approach? Or had it been this sweet little charmer who, with a single smile, could move mountains and melt hearts?

She allowed herself to study the man, who looked so different now that he was asleep. The harsh planes and angles of his face softened into a smile. Those long dark lashes cast mysterious shadows over his cheeks. A strand of dark hair fell rakishly over his forehead and she had an almost overwhelming desire to brush it aside.

Instead she leaned forward and touched a hand to

Brittany's forehead. The medicine had done the trick. The fever was gone, at least for the time being. She was sleeping peacefully.

Heather tiptoed out of the room and quietly closed the door.

Then she took the time to look around. The rooms reflected the man and child who lived here. A stack of books rested on the table beside a comfortable chair, the titles reflecting a wide range of interests: *Law and Civil Disobedience, Understanding the Criminal Mind, How To Explain Death to a Child.*

Heather felt a tug at her heart as she read the last title and glanced at the framed photograph on a shelf. In it Thad stood proudly beside a beautiful blond woman holding a newborn baby who could only be Brittany. The same little turned-up nose, a cap of dark hair and her father's eyes.

Heather moved closer, to study the woman. She could see no trace of her in little Brittany.

She felt such a wave of sadness at the thought of a baby losing her mother at such a tender age.

To distract herself from such thoughts she turned back to the stack of books. There was a smattering of fiction novels, and several dog-eared children's bedtime stories.

It pleased her to think about Thad reading to his little daughter. The image of the two asleep in the next room caused her to smile.

Across the room Heather knelt to study a beautiful dollhouse. On closer inspection she realized it had been handmade, the shell constructed of wood. The interior walls had been papered and painted, the floors covered with colorful rugs. It was fully furnished, even down to the pictures on the walls, which looked as though they'd been cut from magazines and then framed with tiny ribbons.

"The only thing she wanted for her birthday was a dollhouse."

At the sound of Thad's voice Heather looked up to see him standing in the doorway watching her.

"Not like the ones in the stores, but a very special dollhouse that she described to me in great detail every night before she fell asleep. It took me the better part of six months, but I managed to have it finished in time for her birthday."

Heather straightened, feeling suddenly overwhelmed by his presence. "Brittany must have been thrilled."

"Yeah. It's her favorite thing to play with."

"It's so perfect, I'm…speechless."

"Because a big clumsy guy like me could make something so delicate?"

She shook her head. "No, Thad. I'm in awe of you. You seem to have this amazing ability to balance your personal and professional life, despite enormous odds."

He smiled. "The professional life's easy." He pulled the bedroom door closed and took a step closer. "As for the personal life, except for Brittany, there is none."

"Is that the way you want it?"

The way she spoke the words had him going very still. "I've learned that I can't always have what I want."

"And what is it you want, Thad?"

He remained where he was. Afraid to step closer. Afraid that if he did he might do something foolish.

"What I want for myself doesn't matter nearly as much as what I want for my daughter." His tone lowered, softened. "I want that magical kingdom for her. With the flying horse and the puppy that talks people language."

Heather smiled. "That's easy. Any place where her daddy is will become her magical kingdom. As for the horse, she'll be old enough to ride in a few years, and she'll feel like she's flying once she takes the reins and sets off by herself across a field."

"Okay. How about the talking dog?"

She laughed. "Have you ever seen a child and a puppy? Put them together and within minutes they're speaking the same language."

Thad shook his head. "Do you always make everything seem this easy?"

"Yeah." Because he refused to move toward her,

she took a step closer, and saw the guarded look come into his eyes. "Maybe because you try to make things so difficult."

"What's that supposed to mean?"

"This." She reached out a hand to touch him and felt him flinch as her palm rested against his cheek. "I think you and I want the same thing, Thad. But every time I get too close, you push me away." She glanced at the hand he'd already brought to her shoulder, in an attempt to hold her at arm's length. "You've got this wall around you. I think it's really around your heart. Maybe because it got hurt in the past, and you've decided not to let it happen again."

"If that's the case, what are you doing here?"

Her smile bloomed. "I've never been afraid of walls. I was always this tomboy who could climb over, or tunnel under. And if that didn't work, I'd just take a sledgehammer to it and force my way through."

He was watching her so intently she could feel the heat begin to burn her cheeks. "And what happens if you break through and don't like what you find on the other side?"

"I guess I'll just have to find out, won't I?"

"I can't let you, Heather. A woman like you." His voice lowered, thickened, as though talking to himself. "I'd hurt you. I might not want to, but I wouldn't be able to help myself. I can't help being who and what I am, any more than you can. I'm all wrong for you.''

''I don't understand.'' The pain of rejection darkened her eyes. ''What do you see when you look at me, Thad?''

He knew he would hurt her. But it had to be done. Then maybe she would understand and give up this foolishness. ''What do I see? That's easy. Silk and lace. Private schools and country clubs. Pretty boys in Armani suits chasing after you from the time they were old enough to feel their hormones raging. And you, oblivious to the string of broken hearts, leading them on until you grew tired of them.'' He saw her look of surprise. ''Now try to tell me I'm wrong.''

She shook her head, sending her honey hair dancing. ''You're not. I am all those things. Or at least I was. But you missed a couple of others.''

''Such as?''

She took a step back, breaking contact. But even as her heart felt battered, she lifted her chin, determined not to let him see how much he'd hurt her with that accurate description of the way she'd been. ''I'm also a girl with a good mind who wanted more than the superficial things her friends were chasing after. A free spirit who hated the gilded cage she'd been born to. Someone who learned early in life that she could do whatever she set her mind to. And I will." Her voice lowered to a breathy sigh. "Though I guess it won't be with you."

She turned away. "Good night, Thad. I'm glad I was able to help with Brittany. By the way, those fevers aren't usually serious in little ones. It could be something as simple as a virus going around the neighborhood. Or a cold. If it doesn't come back, you're out of the woods."

She picked up her purse and started toward the door. Before she could pull it open he was across the room in quick strides. His hand closed over hers on the doorknob.

"That's what the doctor said. So what makes you so knowledgeable about kids?"

She shrugged and kept her back to him. "When I worked as a camp counselor, we had to know a smattering of health and first aid."

"So you told me." He lifted his hand away from hers. "I told you what I saw in you. But you haven't told me what you see when you look at me."

"That's easy." She turned. "I see a strong man. Strong enough to pick up the pieces after the death of his wife and raise their little girl alone. An honest, decent man in a world that makes it easy to be otherwise. With a clever mind. Clever enough to fashion a dollhouse for his daughter's birthday, while putting in full days climbing the ranks of the department. A man who's maybe a little too proud sometimes, especially when he needs help and refuses to ask for it.'' She took a deep breath and stared up into his eyes. "You're a good man, Thad Law."

He shook his head. "No I'm not. I've seen things you can't even imagine. Misery. So much of it, I could hardly breathe because the stench of it filled my lungs. Crimes so violent I'll never be able to speak of them. I've seen every kind of deviant behavior man can think of. I'm not nice, Heather. This job, this world I live in, changes a man. There are dark places inside me you can never go. And if you could glimpse them, you'd run screaming back to your safe, sheltered mansion.''

She lifted her chin. "I'm not afraid, Thad. Not of you. And not of your life.''

"You ought to be, dammit.'' Without thinking, he grabbed her arm. His eyes were suddenly hot and fierce, and despite her protest, she felt a tingle of fear. "If you knew what I was thinking right now, you'd be shocked right down to the toes of those designer sandals. And you'd want to do a whole lot more than just slap my face.''

Instead of pulling away she lifted her finger to his lips. "Why don't you tell me? Or better yet, show me.''

He groaned and closed his hands roughly over the tops of her arms, intending to push her away. But the minute he came in contact with her flesh, he felt the rush of need that seemed to take over his will.

He dragged her against him, his face in her hair. "You don't want me, Heather."

"I do." She said it so simply, he felt a tiny crack in his armor.

Still, one of them needed to be strong. To be sensible. "I can't be gentle."

"I don't need you to be gentle." She pressed her lips to his throat. "I just need you, Thad."

He was helpless to fight this. He could feel his body straining toward hers. Could feel himself slowly slipping under her spell. Still he had to give her one last chance to run. "I can't make you any promises."

"I won't ask for any."

"Then you're a fool. Because right now, this minute, I'd give you the moon if you asked."

And then his mouth was on hers, like a man desperate to take. His arms came around her, pressing her so firmly against him, he could feel her heartbeat inside his own chest.

Still it wasn't enough. He wanted her. All of her. With the kind of madness born of desperation.

Whatever fears he harbored were forgotten. Whatever differences divided them were put aside.

For now, for tonight, he would give in to the madness that drove him and deal with his demons when the storm of passion had run its course.

Ten

He tasted her. Devoured her. Drawing in all that sweet, exotic flavor that seemed so unique to her.

Too rich for my blood.

The thought came back to haunt him and he knew, if he'd taken time to think this through, he'd have been wise to send her packing.

But he wasn't wise. He was a fool. One who couldn't think, couldn't reason. All he could do now was let the tide of insanity carry him, and savor the moment.

Framing her face, he stared down into those wide blue eyes. "I'll try to be gentle, Heather. But I've wanted you for so long." He pressed soft kisses to her eyelids, her cheek, the tip of her nose, forcing himself to taste, when what he wanted was to feast. "So very long."

His tongue tangled with hers, teasing, arousing, until she sighed from the pure pleasure of it. He lingered over the kiss, as though he'd found a rare treasure worth much more than gold.

Heather sighed, drinking in the dark, male taste of him. His admission that he wanted her, and had for a long time, went straight to her head. His lips were more potent than whiskey. His hands, those big clever hands, brought such pleasure as they moved over her. And his eyes. Those midnight-blue eyes were mesmerizing. Each time she looked into them, she could see herself reflected there. It was the most erotic sensation to see his passion, his needs and desires, so clearly in his eyes.

Just as she began to relax he brought his mouth to her ear. With his teeth he lightly nipped at her lobe before darting his tongue inside. She chuckled at the sweet sensations that rippled through her. But a moment later her laughter became a moan of desperation when he began trailing hot wet kisses along the smooth column of her throat.

She knew if she were a cat she'd be purring. She arched her neck, giving him easier access. He ran light, feathery kisses across her shoulder, over her collarbone. But when he brought his mouth lower, she clutched at his shoulders, afraid that at any moment her trembling legs might fail her.

He pressed her back against the closed door and, with his mouth on hers, kissed her until she couldn't seem to get her breath. When at last he lifted his head she struggled to take air into her starving lungs.

"Last chance," he said abruptly. "If you want out of this, Heather, I won't stop you."

Even as the words slipped from his mouth he wanted to call them back. But it was too late. All those years as a cop had taught him to put everyone else's needs before his own.

For several seconds all he heard was the sound of her ragged breathing. His heart forgot to beat as he waited, wondering what he'd do if she turned away. He'd beg, he'd crawl, he'd die to keep her here with him. If she walked away now he'd go mad with this need that was heating his blood, clouding his mind, battering his senses.

She tossed her head, feigning a boldness she didn't quite feel. "You're not getting rid of me so easily, Thad. I told you. I'm in all the way."

"That's good." He took in several deep draughts of air, hoping to calm his ragged heartbeat. "I wasn't sure I could let you go."

With his eyes steady on hers he brought his hands

to the ends of her gauzy shirt and tugged it over her head before tossing it carelessly aside.

He'd known she would wear silk and lace next to her skin. But the anticipation was nothing like the reality. Seeing that cool, pale silk against her sun-bronzed skin had him thoroughly aroused. He was frantic to tear away the silk and lace, tossing aside the remnants before letting his gaze burn slowly over her.

She looked, in the lamplight, like some beautiful gilded creature that he'd simply imagined. How was it possible for any woman to be this lovely? All that honey hair and golden skin, and the most amazing body. The kind of woman a man spun fantasies around. Like some lush actress far removed from reality.

"Heather." He whispered her name like a prayer and felt her shiver. "You're so beautiful, you take my breath away."

He lowered his head to her breast, his tongue slowly circling until she gasped and clutched at him. He took one erect nipple into his mouth, suckling until she called out his name on a sob. Still he continued the sweet torture, moving from one breast to the other until she thought she would surely go mad.

She was forced to hold on tightly, afraid of falling. But as her world settled again, she became desperate to touch him the way he was touching her.

She struggled with the buttons of his shirt, nearly tearing them off in her haste. When she slid it from his shoulders she moved her palms over his muscled chest, loving the feel of his flesh against hers.

How long she'd wanted to touch him like this. The thought of that hard, toned body had kept her awake so many nights.

On a little sigh she brought her lips to his chest, running openmouthed kisses through the crisp hair. She felt such unbearable excitement as she traced the taut muscles, then moved lower to the flat planes of his stomach, while her fingers fumbled with the snap at his waist until she had him out of the last of his clothes.

Her touch had him wild with need.

Before she had a chance to think he untied her slacks and tugged them over her hips.

His smile was quick and dangerous when he caught sight of the lace thong. "I'm so glad you're wearing that. Did you know it's been one of my fantasies?"

"Then I'm happy to oblige, Detective. In fact, I rather like the idea of being part of your erotic dreams."

Her smile faded when he tore it aside and found her, hot and moist. Without warning he took her on a wild, frantic climb to the first peak, and then over.

But instead of giving her time to recover, he took her again until she was gasping for breath.

"Thad." Her eyes were glazed, her throat burning, as though she'd just run a marathon.

He took her hands in his and lowered her to the floor. With their clothes beneath them they lay, lost in a world of such hard, driving need, the rest of the world seemed to have slipped away.

A gentle rain had begun to fall, dancing against the windows. Neither of them took any notice. Somewhere down the street a car's horn sounded. They didn't hear it. The room was so quiet they could feel each ragged breath, sense each thunderous heartbeat.

They lay locked in an embrace, their bodies slick, the heat of passion rising up between them, threatening to engulf them. His hands tangled in her hair and he drew her head back to stare into her eyes.

"Please, Thad." She hated the note of pleading in her voice, but the need was so great, she could hardly bear it.

"Not yet. There's so much more I want to show you. So much more to give." He covered her mouth with his in a kiss so savage it startled her. For a moment she drew back, startled by the darkness she could taste in him.

Then, as he drew out the kiss, she became so caught up in it, she felt herself sliding with him into the darker side of passion. The need was so intense, so all-consuming, there was nothing she wouldn't do for release.

They rolled across the floor, each driving the other to a new level of madness. One minute she was on top of him, driving him wild with need. The next he moved over her with teeth and lips and tongue, driving her higher, then higher still, keeping what she craved just out of reach.

She clutched at him, touching him as he was touching her. And with each touch he felt the madness rise up and claw at him, fighting to be free.

His body was alive with need. A need that only she could satisfy. And still he held back.

Now there was no tenderness as he feasted on her body. His lips moved from one breast to the other, nibbling and suckling until she moaned and writhed beneath him.

She arched toward him, her hands fisting in the clothes beneath her, while he slowly drove her beyond madness. Though she could hear a voice screaming in her head, her voice was reduced to a hoarse whisper. The only word she could speak was his name.

He struggled to hold back his needs for a minute more as he brought his mouth down her body. He felt her stiffen, and knew that he was taking her to an even darker place. A place she'd never been.

This was how he'd wanted her, how he'd dreamed of her. His. Only his. The touch she craved was his. The only name on her lips was his as he took her up, again and again, until she was blind with need.

"Heather."

He saw her eyes open, watched as she struggled to focus through the red-hot mist of passion that clouded her vision.

And then, as he entered her, she rose up and wrapped herself around him, matching his strength with her own. She moved with him, climbed with him until they seemed to break free of the bonds of earth and fly, soaring among the stars. As they reached the moon they seemed to splinter, before exploding into the most amazing shower of light.

It was a journey unlike anything they'd ever known before.

As they drifted down to earth, his lungs were filled with the fragrance of crushed roses. It was, he knew, a perfume that would forever remind him of this enchanted night, and this amazing woman.

"Are you all right?" Thad's mouth was still pressed to her throat.

"Um-hmm." It was all she could manage.

Heather felt as if something cataclysmic had just happened. As if she'd come as close to dying as it was possible in this life. And that in a single instant she'd been reborn a new woman. A woman who was totally, completely satisfied.

She'd never experienced anything like this. There had been nothing in her life to compare. Was it because of her strong feelings for him? Or was it merely because he was such an incredible lover?

He levered himself above her, easing his weight from her. "Am I too heavy?"

"Um-hmm."

His smile was quick. He studied the way she looked, her eyes still heavy-lidded with passion, her lips still moist and swollen from his kisses. "Is that all you're going to say?"

"Um...I don't think I can manage anything more."

"It was that good?"

She touched a finger to his mouth. "If it was any better, I'd be floating on the ceiling."

He felt a wave of relief. The truth was, he'd never felt anything even close to this before. He'd worried that he'd been so wrapped up in his own pleasure, he'd neglected hers. But now, to learn that she'd experienced it as well had his heartbeat returning to normal.

He rolled aside and drew her close. "I'm sorry about the floor."

"The floor?" For a moment his words didn't register. When they did, she seemed surprised to find herself lying near the door, with only their clothes as a cushion. "I hope you intend to carry me to your bed the next time."

"What makes you think there'll be a next time?"

She sat up, tracing a finger through the mat of dark hair on his chest. "Five dollars says you can't keep away from me."

His eyes narrowed. "Such humility."

She merely laughed. "And to make it more interesting, I'll bet you double or nothing it'll happen before morning."

"Does this mean you're planning on staying the night?"

In reply she bent over him, running light, feathery kisses down his throat, over his chest, and then lower, to his stomach.

She felt his muscles contract as he fisted a hand in her hair. "No fair. You're not playing by the rules."

"I didn't know there were any. I thought all was fair in love and war."

"And which is this?"

She gave a delighted laugh. "It's definitely not war. Though I do feel a bit bruised."

The sound of her laughter wrapped itself around his heart until he thought he might burst from so much happiness.

"Well, then." He got to his feet and lifted her in

his arms. "I think if we're going for seconds, we should do it in the comfort of a bed."

She wrapped her arms around his neck and buried her lips in his throat. Against his flesh she whispered, "What about our bet?"

He could feel the fire race straight to his loins. "Lady, with you all bets are off."

"What's this?" Heather looked up when Thad entered, carrying a tray. She had slipped on his shirt, rolling the sleeves to her elbows. "I thought you were checking on Brittany."

"I was. She's sleeping as peacefully as an angel. Whatever is in that medicine, it did the trick. There's no trace of fever."

"That's wonderful. And this?" She indicated the tray.

"A little snack." He set it on the night table and lifted off a napkin to reveal some wedges of cheese and slices of salami, and a chunk of sourdough rye bread, as well as two cups of steaming herbal tea.

"Umm." She piled some cheese and salami on the bread and took a bite, then offered it to him as he climbed into bed beside her. "That's good."

"Yeah." He couldn't help grinning. "I figured I'd better feed you so you could keep up with me."

"Keep up with you?" She arched a brow. "Just

what did you have in mind when we're through eating?''

"I thought I might—" he took a second bite before passing it back to her "—tear off that shirt and nibble my way from your toes to your nose."

"Oh, my." She touched a hand to her heart. "I'm in bed with a poet."

"Not exactly." He studied her over the rim of his cup. "Though I do feel poetic whenever I look at you. Like right now." He set aside the cup and tucked a lock of her hair behind her ear, allowing his big hand to linger on her cheek. "I still can't believe you're here with me. I keep thinking I'll wake up and find out it's all been some wild dream."

"If it is, then I'm dreaming, too."

"Did you ever have one this real?"

She shook her head.

"So, you're saying it's real?"

She lifted both her hands to his face and stared up into his eyes. "This is real. Only this." She leaned forward to touch her mouth to his.

He felt the sudden jolt to his system and wondered that, even now, after hours of lovemaking, she could still have this effect on him.

His eyes narrowed on her. "Have I told you how much I like you in this shirt?" He slid it from her shoulders and brought his mouth to her throat. "Or how much I like you out of it?"

Her laughter suddenly turned into a moan of pleasure.

And then, while the tea cooled, they slipped once more into the dark, murky depths of passion.

"Is that a bump on your nose?" In the half-light of early morning, Heather leaned up and touched a fingertip to Thad's nose. As dawn began to color the sky, they lay together, too excited by the wonder of their newly discovered joy to sleep. All night they had loved, then slept, then awakened to love again. Each time they discovered something new about the other.

"Yeah. I broke it in a fight years ago."

"A fight? Was this in the line of duty?"

"Hardly." He gave a short laugh. "It was back in high school. I was a tough kid. Always fighting."

"Why?"

"Probably to prove that I was just like the other guys."

"I don't understand. Why did you need to prove that?"

"Because my dad was a cop. Always policing my friends, looking for any sign of drugs or alcohol. I just thought I had to show everybody I was a tough guy. And I was."

"I bet you played a lot of sports."

"Football, soccer and the wrestling team all four years." He saw her grin and arched a brow. "What?"

"I'm not surprised. You look like the football, soccer, wrestling type."

"And what type were you? The cheerleader?"

"Hardly. I couldn't stand to be on the sidelines. I had to be involved. I was on the swim team, the tennis team, and even played on the golf team in college."

"Why am I not surprised?"

"Well, you didn't expect me to say the wrestling team, did you?"

He laughed. "I don't know. You learn some really interesting holds. Want me to teach you a couple?"

"I think I'll pass." Heather touched a fingertip to the scar on his left cheek. "Is this another trophy from your high-school days?"

He shook his head. "That's from my rookie cop days when I came up against a dope-head who'd just slit his wife's throat and wanted to do the same to me."

"Oh, Thad." Heather brushed her lips over the scar. "You could have been killed."

"Yeah. It comes with the badge." He felt the way her hair brushed his face and wondered again at the feelings she'd awakened in him. In the space of one night in her arms he felt as if he could take on all the problems of the world and solve them single-handed.

He gathered her against him and nibbled her ear. "I've got a great idea."

"You do?" Her voice was muffled against his throat, sending splinters of fire and ice along his spine. "What?"

"Let's wrestle. I'm dying to teach you a couple of my moves."

"Great. I'm dying to learn them."

They were still laughing as they came together.

Eleven

"**O**h, no. Did I fall back asleep?" Heather sat up in bed, shoving hair out of her eyes. "I meant to check on Brittany."

"I just did." Thad leaned over and kissed her, then with one hand drew her close and kissed her again, slowly and thoroughly. "She's still asleep. And no trace of the fever."

"Oh, that's such good news." Heather wondered at the way her blood had already begun to heat. Even now, after an entire night together, all Thad had to do was touch her, and the need for him was pulsing through her veins like a drug. "I suppose I should get going."

"So soon?" He couldn't hide the disappointment in his tone. "Why do you have to go?"

"I thought you'd want me gone before Brittany wakes up." She touched a finger to the little frown line between his shaggy brows. "So she won't start asking questions."

"What kind of questions? Heather, she's only four."

"But she's a very smart little girl." She looked up at him. "Won't she find it strange that I spent the night in her daddy's bed?"

"She might. If she has any questions, I'll answer them the way I always have. As honestly and directly as a four-year-old can understand. But I don't know how she'll react. It's not something she's seen before."

That admission, no matter how accidental, had Heather's heart doing a quick free fall. It confirmed what she'd suspected, that Thad Law was no womanizer.

Before she could remark, he added, "But this much I know. Brittany trusts you and accepts you without reservation. I don't think she's likely to give it a thought. Now, how about some breakfast?"

She nodded. "All right. But first, I hope we can salvage my clothes. I didn't bring anything to change into."

He brought his hand from behind his back and

deposited her clothes on the bed. "I think they're intact, though I wouldn't swear to it. I'm afraid I was just a little out of control at the time I took them off you."

As he turned away he said, "I'd love to stay and watch you dress. In fact, it's another of my fantasies. But I need some coffee."

"Oh, coffee. You just said the magic word." She climbed out of bed and started toward the shower. "Make enough for two. I'll be there in ten minutes."

She made it in five. And Thad marveled that within minutes she managed to look as fresh and beautiful as if she'd spent the day at a spa. Her skin glowed with that wonderful luminous quality. Her hair, damp from the shower, was a glorious tangle of waves. He was gratified to note that her blouse and slacks seemed none the worse for his behavior of the previous night.

He held out two boxes of cereal. "You have a choice of Cinnamon Circus Animals or Sugared Xs and Os."

"Oh, I love cinnamon." She filled a bowl and was just devouring her breakfast when Brittany came walking out.

When the little girl caught sight of Heather she gave a delighted squeal and flew into her arms.

"You're here." She turned. "Look, Daddy. Look who's here."

"Yeah. I see." He winked at Heather. "Isn't this a grand surprise?"

"Uh-huh." Brittany climbed up on a chair. "Are you eating some of my Cinnamon Circus Animals?"

"Yes, I am. Is that all right with you, Brittany?"

The little girl nodded, then called to her father, "I'll have what Heather is having, Daddy."

"I thought you might." He placed a bowl in front of her and handed her a spoon. "How are you feeling, sweetie?"

"Oh, I feel fine, Daddy." Brittany turned to Heather and launched into an animated conversation.

"I remember seeing you last night," Brittany said around a mouthful of cereal. "You told me funny stories and kept me from being afraid. And you kept Daddy from being afraid, too."

"Well, sometimes when we're afraid, it helps to have a friend around, doesn't it?"

"Uh-huh. Daddy's my best friend," the little girl said simply.

"You don't know how lucky you are to have a friend like your daddy, honey."

The little girl smiled suddenly. "You can share if you want, Heather. Would you like Daddy to be your best friend, too?"

Heather stared hard into her bowl, avoiding Thad's eyes. "I'd like that, honey."

Thad listened in silence. It all seemed so normal, so right, somehow to have his daughter chattering like a magpie to this woman who looked so relaxed in his kitchen. Eating, of all things, Cinnamon Circus Animals.

"Do you have to work today, Daddy?" Brittany looked up from the table.

"Not today, honey. It's Saturday."

"Oh good." She clapped her hands. "That means we can go shopping, and then to the park."

"Is that what you always do on Saturday?" Heather sat back, sipping strong black coffee.

"Uh-huh. Don't we, Daddy?"

"Yep. Whenever I don't have an emergency at the station." He ambled across the room and took a seat at the table, stretching out his long legs.

"Can Heather come with us?"

"If she wants to."

They both glanced at her, waiting for her answer.

She set down her cup and gave them both a smile. "I wouldn't miss it."

Brittany slurped up the last of the milk in her bowl before grabbing Heather's hand. "Will you help me get dressed?"

"Sure thing." With a last glance at Thad, she allowed herself to be led to Brittany's room.

For the next half hour the apartment was filled with whispers and giggles as the two went through the closet and decided what the little girl should wear.

Heather couldn't stop herself from fantasizing of this as their first family outing.

"Oh, Daddy." Brittany was perched on Thad's shoulders as they walked through the gathering shadows toward home. She polished off the last of her ice cream, then wiped her hands and mouth on the dampened wipe that Heather passed her. "This has been the best day."

Heather was taking her time with her cone, licking each little drop. When she looked up, she realized that Thad was watching, and that with every sensuous movement of her tongue his eyes darkened, his look grew more intense.

She polished off her cone before tucking her hand in Thad's. The heat from his touch was like an inferno. Or was it her own body temperature that had gone up several notches?

She glanced up at Brittany. "What did you like the most?"

"The swings in the park. Especially when I was so high I was flying."

Heather nodded. "That was fun."

"And the movie."

"Who was your favorite character?" Thad asked.

"Goofy."

They all laughed.

"Mickey was mine," Thad said.

"I agree with Brittany." Heather saw the way the little girl was yawning. "I think I liked Goofy best."

"I liked the piz'ghetti afterward, too." The little girl announced.

"Yeah. And the pizza and the salad and the gallons of soda we put away." Heather patted her stomach. "I think I've had enough to get me through the next hour or two."

Thad shot her an admiring glance. "I've never known a woman to eat so much."

"I was just trying to keep up with you."

"Oh. Is that what you were doing? I thought maybe we were having a race, and you were determined to become a marathon eating machine."

She put a hand on her hip. "You're going to pay for that remark, Detective Law."

He shot her a devilish look. "I hope that means you're going to punish me."

She grinned. "In your dreams."

He leaned close. "You'd be very shocked at the content of my dreams since I met you, Ms. McGrath."

"You think so?" She lowered her voice. "Maybe I wouldn't be as shocked as you think."

"And why is that?"

"Because I've had a few dreams of my own since I met you, Detective. But I have to say, reality is much sweeter than any dream."

"Oh, yeah. I echo that." He saw her glance up at Brittany, then touch a finger to her lips.

"I think we wore her out. She's sound asleep."

"I'm glad that nasty fever's gone," he said. "I guess you and the doctor were right."

When they reached the door of his apartment he handed Heather the key while he slipped his daughter from his shoulders, cradling her gently in his arms. Once inside he carried the little girl to her room, where he and Heather undressed her and tucked her into bed.

They stood side by side staring down at the sleeping child.

"She looks just like an angel," Heather said softly.

"I know. I'm always struck by the fact that someone as rough as me could have produced someone as perfect as this."

"She is perfect." Heather linked her fingers with his. "And so is her daddy."

As they stepped from the room and closed the door, he dragged her into his arms and covered her mouth with his in a kiss so hot, so hungry, she could feel the heat searing her flesh, dissolving her bones.

"I want you, Heather." He growled the words against her mouth. "Here. Now."

She could hardly speak. "And I want you."

"I've been thinking of you, of this, all day long."

The look in his eyes was so fierce, she felt her heart stutter. But she kept her eyes steady on his as he tore away her clothes and took her with all the frenzy of a wild summer storm.

"What was your life like before, when your wife was alive?"

"My work was pretty much the same as it is now."

It was well past midnight. As they had the previous night, Thad and Heather had loved and talked and managed a little sleep before waking again.

Now they lay in the dark, snuggled comfortably together.

When he didn't offer anything more, Heather tried again. "I saw her picture on the shelf in the living room. I've been trying to see something of her in Brittany. But all I see is you."

She felt him give a hiss of impatience.

"I'm sorry. I shouldn't have brought up the subject. If it's painful for you to talk about her..."

"I'm...not used to talking about Vanessa."

It was the first time Heather had heard her name.

"Did Vanessa have any family? Does Brittany

have grandparents, and aunts and uncles and cousins?''

"None. Vanessa was an only child. She and her parents were traveling in their private jet when it went down."

"Oh, Thad." She reached out a hand in the dark and touched his cheek.

His voice sounded distant, disinterested. "They flew often. Palm Beach. Puerto Vallarta. Palm Springs. Vanessa's father was on the board of several charities. They felt it necessary to put in an appearance as often as they could. As soon as Brittany was born, Vanessa returned to the role of hostess. She was gone as often as she was home. Brittany was much more comfortable with her nanny than she was with her mother."

Though it was too dark to see his face, Heather knew by the tone of his voice that he was frowning.

"What happened to the nanny?"

"She was a gift from Vanessa's parents. Not exactly something I could afford on my salary."

"As an only grandchild, Brittany must have been left quite an inheritance."

"It's in trust. She'll start receiving it at twenty-one."

"And you? Where did you fit into Vanessa's lifestyle?"

"I didn't. I often wondered why Vanessa married

me. What could she have possibly seen in me? I not only didn't travel in her circle, but I'd made it plain that I wouldn't be willing to change.''

"But you married her. You must have seen something in her you admired.''

"Yeah.'' He gave a sigh. "What man wouldn't be flattered by her attentions? She was a stunner. Beauty. Class. I was so dazzled, I couldn't think. We flew to Vegas within days of meeting, and returned home to receive a healthy dose of reality. When she discovered that she was expecting a baby, I was on a cloud. But all she could think about was losing her figure. From then on she spent more time with her family than with me.'' His tone lowered. "I got the news of the crash while I was on a homicide investigation. I couldn't even get home to be with my baby until almost a day later.''

"Oh, Thad.'' Heather reached out for him and pressed her mouth to his forehead. "I'm sorry.''

As always he felt the jolt of her touch and marveled at it. "What for?''

"For you. For Brittany. For Vanessa. And I'm sorry I asked you. It's made you sad to talk about it. I can hear the sadness in your voice.''

He gathered her into his arms. "It's all in the past now. And I'm not sad. How can I be sad when you're here?'' He covered her mouth with his and lost himself in the wonder of her.

As he did, he was aware that he meant what he'd just said. For every moment he spent with Heather, the bitterness of the past seemed to be melting away, like mist in the warmth of the sun. The prison wall he'd built around his heart was crumbling. With this woman he felt new and free. Like a man reborn.

He ignored the tiny fear hovering at the edges of his mind, that this was all happening too fast. How could there be anything wrong, when it all felt so right?

"What are you doing?" Heather awoke to find Thad leaning up on one elbow, staring at her with that intense look she always found so unnerving.

"Just looking at you."

"Why?" She sat up and lifted a hand to sweep the hair from her eyes, unmindful of the fact that she was wearing nothing.

He shook his head. "I can't quite wrap my mind around the fact that I have a princess in my bed."

That had her chuckling. "Royalty? Hmm. I might learn to like that. Think I can get you to do my bidding?"

"Without question. One haughty look from those cool blue eyes and I'm your slave."

"Oh, I do like this. Kiss me at once, slave."

He brushed his lips over hers.

She sighed. "More. I want more."

He kissed her again, lingering over her lips, drawing out all the flavor, all the sweet fresh taste of her, until they were both sighing.

She wrapped her arms around his neck. "Oh, Detective Law, I do like the way you kiss."

"Not bad for a cop, you mean?"

"I was thinking more along the lines of a prince."

"I'd never be mistaken for royalty."

With a fingertip she traced the outline of his lips. "No, you wouldn't. Anyone can see you're a cop."

"Because of my scars?"

She shook her head, keeping her eyes on his. "Because of the way you walk. The way you talk. The way you listen and probe and dissect. You're straight arrow, Thad. You may not know it but men are respectful in your presence. They know they're in the company of a good, honest man. Your father's influence ran deep."

He drew back, deeply touched by her words.

"Now if you'll excuse me." She sat up and stepped out of bed, padding naked from the room. Minutes later she returned with a basket of clean clothes.

"What are you doing?"

She smiled. "I had to wash my things last night, so I washed yours and Brittany's, too."

His voice was gruff. "You didn't have to do our laundry."

She slipped into her silk bra and lacy thong. "I don't mind. I've never understood the big deal about laundry. You push a few buttons, you fold a few things..." She saw the strange look on his face and paused. "What's wrong?"

He put his hands behind his head and gave her a dangerous smile as he lay back. "Nothing. Just indulging my fantasy. Would you mind putting on the rest of your things? Not that they'll be on for very long. As soon as you're dressed I intend to undress you and get you back into this bed."

It occurred to Heather that she'd never done anything like this before. But as she stepped into her slacks and pulled the opaque top over her head, the look on Thad's face had her heart turning somersaults. She felt dangerous. Reckless. And more than a little wicked.

When, true to his word, he undressed her, she was as aroused as he. And as they came together in a firestorm of passion, she felt her heart overflowing with love for this rough, earthy and very sexy man.

Twelve

Heather walked from the bedroom to find Thad in the kitchen, in jeans and a T-shirt, standing at the stove flipping pancakes. The sight of him always had the same effect on her. He was, quite simply, the most commanding presence she'd ever known. It was impossible to look away from him.

Brittany was seated at the table, looking positively adorable in pink-checked overalls and a pink T-shirt. Her hair, still damp from her bath, was already curling into ringlets that bobbed at her shoulders.

Heather crossed to the table. "You did tell me

you cooked, but I guess I didn't believe you. Until now."

Thad grinned. "Out of necessity, I've become a regular Renaissance Man."

"Heather." Brittany lifted her arms to hug her and Heather scooped her up.

"Umm. You smell good. Did your daddy wash your hair?"

"Uh-huh. He uses baby shampoo so it doesn't sting my eyes. If you want, I'll let you use some, too."

"Thank you, honey. I used whatever your daddy had in his shower. But it doesn't smell nearly as good as yours."

"That's 'cause he's a man." The little girl wrinkled her nose. "Daddy says he doesn't want to use girlie stuff on his hair."

"Yeah." Heather wrinkled her nose in perfect imitation. "It's a guy thing. He's afraid he won't be nearly as tough and macho if he smells too good."

"I'll remind you two females that there's a guy doing the cooking at the moment." Thad neatly flipped several pancakes onto a platter. "So if you want to enjoy your breakfast, say only nice things about men."

Heather put a finger to her lips and the two giggled before sitting down at the table.

As Brittany picked up her fork she said, "Daddy always makes pancakes on Sunday morning."

"Always?" Heather cut the little girl's pancakes into bite sizes before tackling her own.

"Uh-huh. Unless he gets called down to the police station. Then we stop along the way and get something. But it's never as good as Daddy's." Brittany added enough syrup to have them swimming before she took her first bite. "Daddy makes the best pancakes in the world. Don't you, Daddy?"

"That's right." He winked at Heather. "I'm the one who taught her to say that."

He switched off the stove and carried a plate of sausage to the table, then tucked the Sunday newspaper under his arm before filling two cups with coffee.

"Remind me to have an excuse to drop by often on Sunday then," Heather said as she dug into her breakfast. "Because I love pancakes and sausage."

Brittany watched as her father laid out the paper beside his plate. "We don't talk much at Sunday breakfast, though."

"And why is that?" Heather glanced across the table.

"'Cause Daddy likes to read his paper."

"What about you?"

Brittany shrugged. "Daddy says I'm not old

enough to read yet. But when I am, he'll give me part of the newspaper. I wish I could read now.''

"That shouldn't stop you." Heather sorted through the pile of paper until she came to the comics. She folded the colorful section beside Brittany's plate. "Why don't you look at all these silly pictures, and if you find something you like, I'll read it to you."

"You will?" Caught up in a new game, Brittany studied the pictures until she came to a funny-looking dog and cat. "Will you read this one, Heather?''

Minutes later Thad set down his paper to watch as Heather, seated beside his daughter, read her the comics and then explained the jokes.

He lifted his coffee and drank, thoroughly enjoying the sound of laughter filling the room. How had such an ordinary morning taken on this feeling of celebration?

It was Heather, he realized. Whenever she was around, everything seemed to be so much more. More laughter. More enthusiasm. More delight in the simplest of things.

She glanced over and caught him staring. For a moment her cheeks bloomed with color. Then Brittany tugged on her sleeve, and she returned her attention to the comics. When she looked over again,

Thad had picked up his paper and resumed his reading.

She realized that she'd become so aware of him. So in tune with every look he gave her, with every word he spoke. She was even beginning to believe she could influence his thoughts. As if to prove it she continued staring at him and he lowered the paper to glance at her. She smiled. He winked.

And her heart actually fluttered in her chest.

It was a good thing he kept all that charm hidden behind that tough-guy facade. If everyone could see him the way she did, he'd lose his credibility as a cop. And she'd have to lock the doors to keep away the throngs of women eager to have that devilish smile turned on them.

Heather walked outside where Thad and Brittany were waiting to go to the park. As she walked down the steps Thad asked, "What did your uncle say when you told him you were spending another day?"

She smiled and tucked the cell phone in her pocket. "That he wasn't surprised."

As Thad started to pull Brittany in the wagon toward the park, he arched a brow and held his silence. He tried to imagine what Joe Colton really thought about his niece spending the weekend with the cop assigned to his case.

Not that Joe could do anything about it, Thad realized. Heather was a grown woman, able to do as she pleased. And from that independent streak in her nature, he'd be willing to bet she'd been calling all the shots in her life for quite some time now.

Still, it would probably be a lot easier for her family to swallow if she were spending the weekend on some millionaire's yacht.

The mere thought had him frowning.

"There it is again." Heather glanced over.

"There's what?"

"That look. Where were you just then?"

He grinned. "On a yacht."

She laughed delightedly. "How'd you like it?"

He shook his head. "I was getting seasick."

"Have you ever been on a yacht?"

"Once. To handle an investigation. The victim was some rich guy who went over the side. Drowned. It turned out that he'd cheated on his wife and she found out about it."

"So she pushed him over?"

"Either that or he was a lousy sailor. The seas were calm. There were no other craft in the area. And somehow he went over the side and never came up. When we fished him out, he had a lump on his head the size of Fresno. She said he must have hit his head when he fell. Needless to say, her story stretched the limits of credibility."

"So the D.A. didn't buy it?"

"Nobody bought her story. The jury took all of two hours to find her guilty."

"Did she do any time?"

"A couple of years. She had a very exclusive, very expensive law firm. Of course, she could afford it. And I'm sure she'd figured all the angles before she knocked the old guy out and tossed him over the side."

Heather was shaking her head in amazement when Thad had a sudden thought. "Have you ever been on a yacht?"

"Yep."

"Did you get seasick?"

She laughed. "No. As a matter of fact, I'm a very good sailor. But I was pretty bored."

"Bored? On a yacht? Why?"

"It was the company, I guess. We sipped champagne while the crew did all the work, which looked to be much more fun than we were having. The guests were more interested in what everybody was wearing than in the beautiful sunset. And when we docked, my host made an unwelcome pass and found himself, like the guy you investigated, overboard. Fortunately for him, he could swim. I was too furious to even bother looking back to see whether he climbed out by himself or was fished out by his crew."

Thad was laughing so hard he had people in the park turning to see what was so funny. He paused to brush a kiss over Heather's lips. "That does it. I'm never buying a yacht. And if I ever make an unwelcome pass at you, I'd better be prepared for the consequences."

"You got that right, Detective." She held out a hand to Brittany as the little girl climbed out of the wagon. "Come on, honey. Let's go see who can swing the highest."

The two raced toward the swings, leaving Thad to follow more slowly with the wagon.

He felt a glow of happiness at the scene before him as Heather lifted Brittany onto a swing and gently pushed her. The sound of their laughter carried on the breeze, touching his heart as nothing else possibly could. This entire weekend had been like an unexpected gift. And he was feeling as happy as a kid on his birthday.

It was one of those clear, cloudless nights. The moon was a giant golden globe in a sky dotted with millions of twinkling stars.

Brittany, dressed in bunny pajamas, knelt beside her dollhouse, playing quietly.

When Heather stepped out of the bedroom carrying the little girl's soiled clothes, Brittany looked up. "Did you see my dollhouse, Heather? Daddy made it for me."

"I've been admiring it, Brittany." Heather deposited the clothes in a hamper before kneeling beside the little girl. "I see you're rearranging the furniture."

"Uh-huh. Daddy made all the furniture, too." The little girl moved the tiny sofa to a window, then picked up a man doll and placed it there.

"Is the daddy sleeping?" Heather asked.

"No. He's got his eyes closed, but he says that's how all men watch football on television."

"Of course. With their eyes closed." Heather shot a glance at Thad and grinned. "That's how they usually watch the last half of old movies on television, too." She pointed to the flowered bedroom, where Brittany was placing a little girl doll in the bed and covering her with a tiny blanket. "Is she watching television, too? Or does this mean she's getting tired?"

"She's not tired." Brittany stifled a yawn. "She's just resting her eyes."

Heather tried not to smile. "Are you sure about that? She looks awfully tired to me."

"Well," the little girl said hesitantly, "maybe a little."

"Would you like your daddy to tuck you in? That

is, of course, if he can tear himself away from the comfort of his sofa?''

''I guess so.'' Brittany stood and caught Heather's hand. ''Will you come with me and tuck me in, too?''

''Of course.'' Heather glanced around the carefully arranged dollhouse and noticed something. ''Is that all you have? A daddy doll and a little girl doll? Isn't there somebody missing?''

''Uh-huh,'' Brittany said matter-of-factly. ''There was a mommy doll in the package, too, but Daddy said I didn't need her. So I put her away.'' She led Heather into her bedroom and opened a dresser drawer. ''See?''

At the sight of the mommy doll tucked away in a corner of the drawer Heather felt such a wave of sadness she had to swallow the lump in her throat. She tried to imagine what her own life would have been like without her mother's wisdom to guide her.

Heather was grateful when Thad walked in a minute later and started one of his silly bedtime stories.

Soon the three of them were laughing at the antics of Thad's imaginary characters, a zebra, a leopard and an elephant, that lived in Brittany's closet and wore her clothes. By the time they tucked the little girl in, she was sound asleep and they were both smiling.

As they walked from her room Thad linked his

fingers with Heather's. "Can I persuade you to stay one more night?"

She gave him a sly smile. "I don't know. Maybe I ought to go. After all, I think I've seen all your moves by now."

He looked down at their linked fingers and drew her fractionally closer. "I've got a couple of new ones."

"Really?" She could feel her body straining toward his and marveled that, without so much as a kiss, her body was becoming liquid.

"Yeah. I thought we could start with this." He drew her closer and combed his fingers through her hair.

With his eyes steady on hers he said, "And then we could do this." He traced the outline of her lips with his tongue and heard her sharp little intake of breath. But instead of kissing her he continued teasing her, tracing with his tongue the outline of her ear, the curve of her cheek, until she thought she couldn't wait another moment for the press of his lips on hers.

"I like your moves, Detective. But I have a few of my own." She lifted herself on tiptoe and caught his face in her hands, pressing her lips to his.

She heard his hiss of pleasure and stepped back, giving a little cat-smile of satisfaction.

"Not bad," he muttered.

"What do you mean, not bad?"

"I mean that it was pleasant enough, but it was far from award-winning."

"I see." She regarded him through narrowed eyes. "You want my Academy Award performance, do you?" She draped herself against him and wrapped her arms around his waist.

Against his mouth she whispered, "Better fasten your seat belt, Detective Law. You're in for a long and bumpy ride."

She pressed him back against the wall and tangled herself around him before lifting her mouth to his. With a purr of satisfaction she felt his body respond. But she wasn't finished with him yet.

He wanted moves, did he?

She moved, slowly, deliberately, so that every part of her body rubbed his in the most delicious, sensuous way possible. Her lips warmed, softened on his as she melted into him like hot wax to a flame.

"Okay. I give up," he muttered against her mouth. "You win. In fact, for this you deserve the Academy Award."

"But I'm not through, Detective."

His hands were rough, impatient. His body hard and tense and growing hotter by the minute. "Heather, you're killing me." His blood was pumping furiously as she continued tormenting him, making soft, mewing sounds in her throat as she practically crawled inside his skin.

But instead of stopping, she kept it up until he swore and held her a little away, until he could catch his breath.

"Okay. That's it." He swung her into his arms and headed down the hall toward his bedroom.

"But I had more moves to show you."

"You will." He was sweating as he kicked in the door and carried her to the bed. "Believe me, baby, you can show me anything you want." He lowered her to the mattress and covered her lips with his, while the blood roared in his head.

She pressed a hand to his heart and heard the furious pounding that matched her own.

And then, because she'd been the one to start this, she decided she ought to be the one to finish it. Pouring all her love, all her heart, all her soul into it, she rolled over him and took him on the ride of a lifetime.

Thirteen

Heather stepped from the shower and wrapped a towel around herself. Across the room, Thad stood shaving, a towel hanging loosely at his hips. It was such an ordinary thing, and yet so oddly intimate. Maybe that was what she loved about being here. The utter simplicity of it all. A man and a woman going about their daily tasks and taking such joy in them. And the anticipation of knowing that when the day was done they would come together to share a meal, a walk, a bedtime story with a little girl who was such a delight.

Not to mention the loving they shared. It was, she

realized, extraordinary. She'd never known a man like Thad Law. He could be gentle and patient, making her feel like the most cherished woman in the world as he led her through a garden of delights. At other times he could be rough and impatient, taking her to the very depths of darkness and passion, the likes of which she'd never even dreamed.

He was a constant surprise. Silly or serious. Abrupt or thoughtful. And always so loving and patient with his daughter. It was, she realized, the most endearing of all his traits.

She bent at the waist, twisting a towel around her hair before straightening. As she did she caught sight of Thad watching her in the mirror.

There was no denying what she saw in his eyes. Even now, as he prepared for work, he wanted her. It was, to her, more erotic than wealth or prestige or possessions.

She walked up to stand beside him and saw the way his gaze shifted to her reflection. He wiped the last of the shaving cream from his face before turning to her.

"It just occurred to me that I was supposed to spend this weekend finding a sitter for Brittany." He pressed a kiss to her nose. "But I got sidetracked by a beautiful, bewitching creature who stole my brain."

She laughed. "And attacked your body."

"Yeah. That, too. I should feel exhausted. But strangely enough, I feel like I could lick the whole world."

"Pretty dangerous thoughts for a cop. Try not to solve all the crimes of the world in a single day, Superman."

"With someone like you believing in me, I almost think I could." He sighed. "Anyway, here it is Monday and all I've done is play. Which means I still haven't found a sitter for Brittany."

"Oh, yes, you have." She brushed a kiss over his lips. "You're looking at her."

"You can't keep this up, Heather. You're here to help Joe, not to help me."

"If you can go out and solve crimes, I guess I can manage to answer a few faxes and still watch one little girl." She turned away and headed for the bedroom, giving him no time to argue.

Half an hour later, over breakfast, the phone rang. While Heather helped Brittany with her cereal, Thad snatched up the receiver.

Heather heard him say, "Yeah. I can be there in fifteen minutes."

He hung up the phone and turned. "Sorry to run out on you, but I'm needed at the station. There's been an emergency. I guess this solves the question of what we'll do about today. Would you mind taking Brittany with you?''

''Not at all.'' Heather poured juice and handed it to the little girl. ''But you'll need to transfer her car seat to my car.''

He nodded and hurried over to explain to his daughter. ''You're going to the ranch with Heather, honey, while I take care of some business. Then I'll come out there later and get you. Okay?''

''Okay, Daddy. Do I get kisses?''

''You bet.'' He lifted her in his arms, loving the way she wrapped her chubby arms around his neck and lifted her face to him.

When he set her back in her chair she returned her attention to her cereal. Heather walked with him to the door. ''Do I get kisses, too?''

''Yeah.'' His smile was that dark, dangerous one she'd come to love.

He dragged her close and kissed her hard and quick.

''Thanks.'' She touched a hand to her heart. ''I needed that.''

''Not nearly as much as I did.'' He started away, then turned back and drew her close for another kiss, this time lingering over her mouth until she was sighing with pleasure.

Then, before he could get sidetracked, he turned and walked quickly away.

* * *

"Come on, Brittany." Heather lifted the little girl out of the car and turned toward the row of shops in the strip mall.

Though she'd never shopped here, she'd often seen the familiar sign advertising fine coffees. She would surprise Thad with his favorite tonight.

"Where are we going?" Brittany asked.

"Just to that coffee shop. We have time before I have to start work."

As she passed the phone booth she was startled by the sight of her Aunt Meredith inside, gesturing as she spoke into the phone. For a moment Heather paused, wondering why her aunt would be here, miles from home, using a public phone when she had a perfectly good cell phone at her disposal.

Even through the closed door of the phone booth she could hear her aunt's voice raised in anger.

Without a word Heather caught Brittany's hand and hurried past. When they reached the coffee shop she placed her order, then turned and glanced out the window at the figure of her aunt, still gesturing as she spoke into the phone.

Meredith Colton had changed so dramatically over the past years, she was hardly recognizable. She was so different from the sweet, considerate person she'd once been. There had been a time when she'd been Heather's favorite aunt. Now Heather dreaded having to be near her. From what she had observed since arriving at the ranch, even Meredith's own husband and children avoided her.

She glanced at Brittany, innocently waiting for her to pay for her purchase so they could be on their way. She'd once thought that being motherless would be the saddest thing in the world. But now she had just thought of something even worse. Being a mother whose own children couldn't stand to come near.

Patsy's voice was pure ice. "Just answer me this. Have you found Emily or haven't you?"

The voice of Silas "Snake Eyes" Pike was nearly drowned out by static, causing Patsy to mutter a string of curses. "You fool. Can't you even buy a decent phone?"

"Yeah. I could." There was more static before he added, "If you'd pay me enough."

That had her clenching a fist and kicking a foot against the enclosure.

"Now. To answer your question." Pike's voice faded in and out. "I've narrowed my search to Wyoming."

"Why there?"

"Let's just say I have plenty of contacts in low places. After all these years, I've met dozens of snitches. And they tell me the object of my search is in Wyoming."

Patsy paused in her pacing. "That's it? This is your big announcement? Emily is somewhere in the state of Wyoming?"

"That's what I said." His tone was filled with pride.

"In case you haven't noticed, you fool, Wyoming is a very big state. Just where in Wyoming is she?"

"Hey. Stop your yelling. I got this far, didn't I? Don't go getting yourself all worked up in a lather about this. I'll find her. I just need time."

"I don't have much time left. Some damned fool has been wasting all my time with one clever story after another."

"You know what?" His voice turned into a whine. "I'm sick of you calling me a fool. If you don't like the way I work, maybe you should find someone else."

"Maybe I will. Maybe I just will, you little weasel." Her tone sharpened. "Someone who won't bother me with phone calls saying he has the whole state of Wyoming left to search. Maybe this time I'll hire someone who can deliver the goods."

She was rewarded with a quick change in his attitude. "Now wait a minute. I didn't say I couldn't do the job. I can. I will. But it's going to cost you."

"Have I ever quibbled about price?"

He laughed. "Every time we talk. But hey, who's

keeping score? Just wire me some more money. And while I'm waiting, I'll be digging up all I can on sweet little Emily.''

Patsy hastily wrote the address of the town where Silas Pike was staying before hanging up on him.

Patsy frowned. He always wanted more money. But she never got any results. That's what she got for hiring such a loser. But what did she expect from an ex-con who'd spent his whole life in the system, first in foster care after his father beat his mother to death, and then in prison for car theft and armed robbery. He talked a good game, but so far, he had yet to deliver. Maybe what she ought to do was hire a hit man to do away with the slimeball, then pay the hit man a bonus to do away with the infuriating little Emily, as well.

For the first time in more than an hour a smile touched her lips. Oh, how she'd love to follow through on that dream. But the whole thing was simply too preposterous. With her luck, the hit man would probably turn out to be an FBI informant. And then where would she be?

No. She paused and crossed her arms over her chest, staring out the window, tapping a fingernail on her arm. As much as she wanted to be done with this place and be on her own, for now she'd have to sit tight and hope that Pike found Emily soon.

Otherwise, she just might hire a hit man. One who

could be counted on to get the job done right. Or, if Pike made her mad enough, maybe she'd even do the job herself.

Joe Colton studied his niece as she walked toward his desk, holding little Brittany's hand.

"Well, don't you two look bright-eyed this morning."

Heather flushed. "I hope you don't mind that I brought Brittany with me. Thad had to go to the station. He'll be by later to pick up his daughter."

"Now why would I mind two pretty women sharing my office?" Joe winked at the little girl. "I was hoping you'd come for a visit. I picked up another bottle of bubbles over the weekend."

"Bubbles." Brittany clapped her hands. "Can we do it now?"

"How about if we wait until lunchtime? It's such a pretty day we'll eat in the courtyard, and you can chase all the bubbles you want."

"Okay."

Heather set the little girl down before tearing off a fax and placing it on Joe's desk. Then she handed Brittany a pad of paper and several colored markers to play with while she and Joe went over some of the correspondence he wanted answered.

Joe looked up. "I'm going to need a couple of financial reports, sweetheart. Thank heavens they're your specialty. You can do in half an hour what it would take me the whole day to do.''

Heather smiled. ''That's not a problem. Do you need them right away?''

He nodded. ''As soon as possible.''

''I'll run them up on the computer now.''

''Good girl.'' He gave her a wink before glancing over at Brittany and announcing loudly, ''I was thinking I'd like to go to the kitchen for a bowl of strawberries. But I hate to go alone. Do you think anybody would be interested in going with me?''

A little voice chirped, ''I'll go with you, Uncle Joe.''

''What's that?'' He held a hand to his ear. ''Did somebody say they'd like to keep me company?''

He felt a tug on his sleeve and looked down to find Brittany smiling up at him. ''I'll go with you, Uncle Joe.'' She took his hand and said solemnly, ''It's okay if you don't want to go alone. Sometimes when it's late at night and really dark, I don't want to be alone, either. And sometimes even in daylight I'm afraid. My daddy says everybody feels that way sometimes. Even him. And it's okay to ask for help.''

Joe walked with her across the room and yanked open the door. ''Your daddy's a very smart man, Brittany. And you're a lucky little girl to have someone like him.''

As their voices faded, Heather thought about what little Brittany had just revealed. What an amazing man Thad was to deal with all his daughter's fears and all her questions in such a forthright manner.

Brittany may not have two parents, but the one she had was a special man indeed. And more than qualified for the task of raising a bright, lovable and thoroughly delightful little girl.

Heather and Brittany were just going in to dinner when Heather's cell phone rang. She let the little girl go ahead with Teddy and Joe, Jr., as she paused in the doorway to answer her phone.

"Thad." At the sound of his voice she felt the quick flutter of her heart. "I've missed you."

"Yeah. I've missed you, too." His voice lowered. "How's my girl?"

"She's just fine. She's just sitting down with the boys in the dining room."

He chuckled. "I was talking about you."

"Oh." Her smile grew radiant. "I wasn't expecting that."

"Then I'm glad I can still catch you by surprise. Now how's Brittany? Getting to be a handful?"

"Don't be silly. She's been having such a good time. You won't believe it. My uncle bought a fresh bottle of bubbles over the weekend, just so he could see her eyes light up when she chased them across the courtyard.''

"That's great." He was genuinely touched by the way Heather's family had accepted his daughter. He paused, reluctant to ask a favor. Finally he blurted it out. "Would it be too much trouble to keep her there a while longer?"

"Of course not."

"I don't know how late I'll be."

She heard the underlying tension in his tone. "Rough day?"

"Yeah. A homicide across town. Listen, I might not be able to get there until pretty late."

"Then why not let Brittany spend the night?"

He paused, considering. "You wouldn't mind?"

"Of course not. She'll sleep with me. I'll tell her outrageous stories, and we'll giggle together." She lowered her voice, so she wouldn't be overheard. "And we'll both miss you."

"Not as much as I'm going to miss you. I hate going home to an empty apartment."

"You could always climb up to my window and stay here tonight."

"Yeah. And be videotaped by half a dozen security cameras. That would certainly create a buzz around town. I can hear the teasers now. 'Top cop caught in security violation at Colton estate. Juicy details of the scandal at six.'"

"I think you've missed your true calling, Detective Law. You should have been a reporter."

"Yeah. Or maybe a fiction writer." She could hear some of the tension seeping out of his voice. "Hold a good thought, Ms. McGrath."

"You, too, Detective."

"With any luck I'll see you in the morning."

She smiled. "Good night, Thad."

She tucked her phone into her pocket and watched as Brittany proceeded to charm everyone at the table. The little girl would be disappointed when she learned that her father wasn't coming to get her tonight. But she was quite a little trooper. Heather had no doubt they'd both get through the long night and would greet the coming morning with high excitement at the thought of seeing the person they both loved.

The person they both loved.

What an amazing feeling. It was shocking to realize how completely, how utterly she loved Thad Law.

But there it was.

She'd thought she was in love before. But, she realized now, being in love, and loving, weren't the same thing. She was grateful that she'd been able to step back all those other times, because now she was free to appreciate just what she'd found with Thad.

Everything that had gone before in her life had

simply been a prelude to now. A series of steps, leading to this man, and this time in her life.

She couldn't wait to see Thad again and to tell him just how special he'd become.

Fourteen

The streets were dark and deserted as Thad drove home. He parked the car and glanced at his watch. Nearly three o'clock in the morning.

The homicide had been grisly and messy. It was the kind of scene that sickened even seasoned police officers. The worst part, as always, was afterward. It took hours, and sometimes days, to wash away the stench of death. But nothing could erase the images that were seared into his memory.

He unlocked the door and stepped inside, turning on lights as he headed down the hall. By the time he reached the bathroom, he'd managed to peel off his jacket and tie, tossing them on the bed as he passed. He kicked aside his shoes and tore off the rest of his clothes before stepping into the shower. He stood under the hot spray for as long as he could stand it, then stepped out and wrapped himself in a towel.

He hadn't eaten since early the previous morning, but he found he had no appetite. He sank down on the edge of the bed and ran his hands through his hair, thinking about the woman and two little children whose bodies had been tagged and taken away.

As a professional, he ought to be immune to such horrors. But as a father, he would never get used to it. Every time he saw it, he had to deal with the darkness all over again.

He'd told Heather that there were places inside himself that she could never go. And it was true. But he'd glossed over the depth of the darkness. It lay like a cloud over his heart, blotting out the sun. It gripped him with sharp, vicious teeth, dragging him down into a depression so all-consuming, he felt as though he might never climb out.

And it played with his mind.

Unable to sit still, he padded barefoot to the kitchen and grabbed a beer from the refrigerator. As he popped the top he turned and stared around the empty room. Without Brittany's presence, it seemed so empty. Too empty to bear.

And then there was Heather. He'd known, of course, that he'd need her here. But he didn't want her around him when he was like this. He knew he needed to shake off this feeling, before it brought him all the way down, but it had taken hold of him, and in his present mood he didn't have the strength to fight it.

As the mood darkened and deepened, he found himself looking around and trying to see his place through Heather's eyes. He stalked from room to room, his mind crowded with ominous thoughts, his soul heavy.

What had he been thinking, bringing her here? She could fit his entire apartment into a single room at the Colton ranch. And though he hadn't seen her family home in San Diego, he had a pretty good idea of her lifestyle there.

What sort of dreamworld had he been living in? What had ever possessed him to think he could hold the attention of a woman like that for more than a few days?

A woman like that.

She'd been raised in an environment of extreme wealth and privilege. She didn't know what it was to want for anything. A snap of the fingers and it was hers. A new car? A closet filled with designer gowns? A horse? A stable of horses? Hers for the asking.

So why would a princess be interested in a pauper? The answer came to him in a flash. Because she'd never known anyone like him before. To a woman like Heather McGrath, a rough-edged working class cop in her bed would be quite a novelty. A conquest to boast about some day when she was sipping wine with old college friends and talking about the foolish things they'd done in days gone by, before they'd snagged their millionaire husbands. And so she'd set her sights on something she'd never had before.

And he'd been so eager to oblige.

When he thought of the way he'd behaved, like a raging bull in a china shop, he felt like such a fool.

He drained the beer and, needing to do something to vent the anger that was building inside, hurled the empty can against the wall before turning away and heading off to his bedroom.

Even the empty bed seemed to mock him.

He switched off the lights and lay in the dark, praying that the yawning black chasm that was hovering overhead wouldn't swallow him up completely.

It would feel like an eternity while he waited for morning to come.

It was a sunny day in Jackson, Mississippi, as Louise Smith sat back in the lounge chair beside the fountain in her garden waiting for Dr. Martha Wilkes to begin another therapy session.

They had done this often enough that the preliminary session had become routine. First came the litany of words Martha spoke aloud to help her relax. As they began to work their magic she closed her eyes and willed herself into a soothing place where she could empty her mind and be open to the questions put to her by her doctor.

Dr. Wilkes kept her voice cool and dispassionate as she led her patient through what had gradually become their daily ritual. Bits and pieces of the past. Threads in the fabric of the twisted and tortured life of the woman Dr. Wilkes knew only as Louise.

Today would be tougher than most. Dr. Wilkes had been leading her patient toward this destination for quite some time.

"All right now, Louise. I want you to take me back to the day of the accident."

Louise's head turned from one side to the other in a lazy refusal. "I don't want to go there again."

"I know." Dr. Wilkes patted her hand, then leaned back. "But I need you to lead me through the events again. Exactly as you remember them."

Louise's eyes flickered, then closed. Her voice became a monotone. "I was driving to Santa Cruz."

"Do you remember why?"

Louise struggled to find her way through the thick fog that enveloped her mind. "Going to see someone."

"Can you recall who it was?"

"A woman. Dark-eyed. Smiling. Her name…" She thought for just a moment she could hear a voice, but then it was snatched away. "No. Don't recall."

"And you were alone in the car as you drove to Santa Cruz."

"No."

Dr. Wilkes quirked a brow before making a notation in her file. "Are you quite certain of that?"

"Not alone. There was…someone with me."

"A man? Or another woman?"

Louise felt the fog closing in, thicker, darker, and struggled to clear it from her mind. "No. Not a man or a woman."

"A child maybe?" Dr. Wilkes watched the way her patient's face became ravaged.

"Maybe. I can't…recall."

Seeing her agitation, Dr. Wilkes kept her voice deliberately soft. "All right. You were driving. Then what happened?"

"A car coming up behind me. Very fast." Louise's voice became suddenly animated, higher-pitched. "Watch out. We're going to be hit."

"Who are you warning, Louise? Or are you just shouting to yourself?"

"Someone." Highly agitated, she gripped the arms of the chair. "Warning whoever is with me to brace for an accident. Then we're swerving. I'm screaming. At least I think it's my voice. Someone is screaming. We're forced off the road, tires screeching, metal crumpling. Then...darkness." Tears rolled down her cheeks as she shook her head and repeated over and over, "Darkness. Only darkness. And emptiness. So empty inside. And I see..." She let out a piercing scream that sounded more animal than human. "Oh, God I see..."

She dissolved into shuddering sobs.

Alarmed, Dr. Wilkes used the prearranged words that would bring her patient out of her hypnotic trance. She studied the pale quiet woman, wondering at this latest setback.

"I know there are secrets, Louise." Dr. Wilkes took her hand and held it between both of hers. "Painful secrets that are struggling to remain locked away. But we'll learn them together. I know we will."

As her patient walked away she switched on her recorder and spoke in clear, concise words. "Patient still traumatized by vivid recollection of the accident. This latest collapse suggests that we should proceed with great care in order to avoid even more severe shock to her fragile system. Otherwise, she could be lost forever.''

''Hi, Daddy. What are you doing?'' Brittany sat cross-legged in the middle of Heather's bed, holding Heather's cell phone to her ear.

In his room Thad could barely lift his head from the pillow. He moved with the speed of a slug, forcing himself to sit up and swing his legs to the floor. ''How's my girl?''

''Fine, Daddy. Heather just helped me take a bubble bath. In a few minutes we're going downstairs and have breakfast. Will you come over and eat with us?''

He ran his hands through his hair and glanced at the bedside clock. It was seven o'clock, and he'd had less than an hour of sleep. He'd tossed and turned for hours, fighting so many demons, he felt weary beyond belief.

''No, honey. I have to go to the station first. But I'll come by for you this afternoon. Okay?''

She dimpled. ''Okay, Daddy. Do you want to talk to Heather?''

She handed over the phone.

Heather's eyes were dancing as she said in her sexiest voice, ''Good morning, Detective Law.''

There was no sound on the other end of the line.

''Thad?'' She listened, then realized they'd been

disconnected. Puzzled, she dialed again and heard the phone ring and ring.

"That's funny." She shoved the phone into her pocket. "Your daddy must have jumped into the shower. Come on, Brittany. We'll eat now and try him again in a little while."

As they made their way downstairs, Heather thought about the previous morning, when she and Thad had watched each other in the mirror. Just thinking about it had the heat rising to her cheeks.

She couldn't wait to see him again. This time apart made her realize all the more how much Thad Law had come to mean to her. And she intended to tell him so at the first opportunity. As soon as they were alone.

It was midday before Thad finished all of the paperwork involved in the gruesome homicide. The mood among his fellow officers in the squad room was subdued. He picked up his suit jacket and made his way to his car.

As he drove to the Colton ranch his thoughts were filled with doom and gloom. He should have never followed his father into police work. He didn't have the stomach for it. To survive on the streets today, a man needed nerves of steel. Not to mention a hard heart. Instead of criminal law, he should have majored in business or real estate. Now there was a way to make great money without losing his heart and soul to all this misery.

Heather had called him a good man. A straight arrow. What he was, he decided wearily, was a fool. One who gave up way too much in the line of duty and got too little in return.

Heather. He knew she was the real reason for this strange mood. Until she came into his life, he'd never questioned his calling. He was a cop. A good one. It's all he'd ever wanted to do. But now, suddenly, he wanted more. Not for himself, but for Heather.

What was he going to do about her? He was already in over his head. Every day that he allowed this to continue, would only make things worse when she finally walked out of his life. And she would, he was certain, walk away when she decided she'd had enough of this relationship.

It would be better to break it off now. It would be painful. But it would be quick and clean.

Quick and clean.

He clenched his jaw. He was about to take a knife to the heart. The least he could do was to try to make it as bloodless as possible. For both their sakes.

"More bubbles, Heather." Brittany clapped her hands.

"What's the magic word?" Heather held the bottle behind her back.

"Please," the little girl said sweetly.

"Now how could I ever refuse you anything?" With a laugh Heather dipped the wand into the bubble solution and blew a stream of bubbles, sending Brittany chasing after them.

They were both laughing when they caught sight of Thad driving up.

Heather quickly capped the bottle and shoved it into the pocket of her jeans, before scooping up the little girl and racing toward Thad's car. By the time he stepped out they were dashing toward him, calling out greetings.

"Daddy." Brittany held out her arms and Heather passed her over to Thad. "Kisses, Daddy."

"You bet." He pressed her close and gave her a fierce hug before kissing her upturned face. "Oh, I missed you."

"I missed you, too, Daddy. But I wasn't afraid. I slept in Heather's bed and she told me stories until she fell asleep."

"You mean until you fell asleep."

"No, Daddy. Heather fell asleep first. Then I just curled up next to her and slept, too. And today I got to take a bubble bath. Smell me, Daddy. Do I smell like Heather?"

Beside him he heard Heather's sultry laugh, but he kept his attention riveted on his daughter. It wouldn't be wise to look at the person he was about to cut out of his life. Besides, he was afraid if he did, he'd lose his nerve.

He breathed deeply and felt the pain, sharp and swift, at the fragrance of crushed roses. "Yeah. You smell good, honey."

"I know. I like it, Daddy. I smell just like Heather. I told her when I grow up I'm going to look just like her. What do you think, Daddy? Can I look like Heather when I get big?"

"I don't think that's possible, Brittany. You have to look like yourself. Besides, why would you want to look like someone else, when you're so beautiful?"

Her big blue eyes got bigger. "Am I as beautiful as Heather?"

"To me you are."

She rubbed her hands over his hair and pressed her lips to his forehead. "Can we stay for dinner, Daddy? Heather says we've having steaks on the grill."

"That sounds good, honey. But we need to get home."

"Okay. Can Heather come home with us?"

This was what he'd been dreading. And now that it was here he was afraid he wasn't going to handle it very well.

He straightened his shoulders. "I don't think so, honey. Not tonight."

Heather touched a hand to his arm. "Sounds like you've had a bad time of it."

He flinched and drew a little away. "Yeah. I've had better."

Puzzled, she lay a hand over his, only to have him draw back again. Was it her imagination, or was he avoiding her? During this entire exchange he hadn't once looked at her. At first she'd thought it was because he'd missed his daughter so much. After all, they were rarely apart. But now she was getting an uneasy feeling along her spine.

"If things are really bad, you can always leave Brittany here another night."

"No." The protest came out sharper than he'd intended. He glanced up and saw the hurt look in Heather's eyes, then decided to just plow through. "We've imposed on you long enough. It's time to get back to our own lives."

"Imposed?" Now the pain was in her voice as well as in her eyes. "How can you even think such a thing, Thad?"

"How? It's easy. You're young and beautiful and you have your whole life ahead of you. The last thing you need is to be tied down with a bad-tempered cop and his kid. As for Brittany and me, we're a team. We don't need anybody except each other." He turned to his daughter, to avoid the mix of pain and confusion in Heather's eyes. "Isn't that right, honey?"

"Uh-huh." The little girl looked from her dad to the young woman beside him. "But why can't Heather come home with us?"

"Because this is her home, honey. This is where Heather belongs."

He could see that his daughter was on the verge of tears. He couldn't stand it if both these females started crying.

He turned toward his car, leaving Heather standing alone.

As he buckled Brittany into her car seat she turned and waved her little hand. "Bye, Heather. See you tomorrow."

He settled himself in the driver's seat and turned the key in the ignition. Without a word he put the car in gear and took off, watching as the figure in the rearview mirror receded until, as the car rounded a curve, she disappeared from sight.

He'd thought it would be like taking a knife to the heart.

He'd been wrong.

It had been worse. Much worse.

He felt as though he'd just ripped his heart from his chest and was now pouring acid on the raw, bloody wound.

Fifteen

Heather stood perfectly still, watching as Thad's car drove away. For the longest time she merely stared, seeing nothing, her mind in turmoil.

What had just happened here?

He'd hugged his daughter. That was to be expected. But he'd studiously avoided her. Avoided touching her. Even avoided looking at her. And the words he'd spoken had seemed to come from someone else. In fact, as she began replaying his words in her mind, they seemed intentionally cruel.

We've imposed on you long enough.

We're a team. We don't need anyone else.

This is where Heather belongs.

…young and beautiful, and you have your whole life ahead of you. The last thing you need is to be tied down with a bad-tempered cop and his kid.

All carefully rehearsed lines guaranteed to let a person down without coming right out and saying so. She ought to know. She'd dumped enough men in her life to know the drill very well.

He'd been saying goodbye. She had become an unwanted intrusion in his well-ordered life. He'd wanted a baby-sitter for his daughter, not a lover in his bed.

She felt her lips quiver and lifted her chin, determined not to cry. She wouldn't waste her tears on Thad Law.

She started toward the house and felt the weight of the bottle of bubble solution in her pocket. Without thinking she pulled it out and stared at it, then was forced to blink hard.

She'd foolishly begun to spin a wonderful fantasy around herself and Thad and Brittany. In her mind's eye she already pictured herself at the little girl's school, going on field trips, helping out with activities. She'd seen Brittany in her high-school yearbook, at the prom, wearing a cap and gown. She'd even imagined Brittany all grown up, walking down the aisle in a wedding gown, and later dancing with her father, and thanking the stepmother who had been there for her through all the years.

What a fool she'd been.

Still clutching the bubble bottle she raced up the stairs and closed herself in her bedroom. There, crossing her arms over her chest, she began to pace. As she did, she turned her wrenching sorrow into something much more manageable. Anger. Now that was something she could deal with.

How dare Thad Law treat her like some teenaged baby-sitter. She may have cared for his daughter, but she'd also done a whole lot more than that. And while it was true that she'd made some moves on him, she hadn't been alone in that regard. He'd made some moves of his own. He'd wanted her every bit as desperately as she'd wanted him. A man couldn't fake that kind of raw, unbridled passion. And the look of love in his eyes had been real, as well. She hadn't imagined it.

She stopped pacing. So, what had happened between yesterday and today to change him?

There had been a homicide investigation. Hadn't he warned her that there were dark places inside him? Had this crime triggered something in him? But what? A need to be alone, to brood in private? But why, if he was feeling hurt or angry, had he decided to stop seeing her altogether?

She began to pace again. Maybe he was simply a

man who was afraid of commitment. Hadn't he said his marriage had been a mistake almost from the beginning?

His marriage.

Heather thought back to what he'd told her. He'd given away so little. In fact, if she hadn't forced the issue, he'd have never mentioned his wife. All he'd said was that she'd been beautiful and blond and wealthy.

Heather paused in midstride and closed her eyes as the pain of realization struck.

Thad saw her as another Vanessa. And their situation as a repeat of the first time. A whirlwind courtship, and then...disaster? Hadn't he hinted that his marriage had been unhappy almost from the beginning? It stood to reason that, because of the similarities, he'd decided to cut his losses and run, figuring if he didn't, she would, sooner or later.

With a speed born of desperation she tore open her bedroom door and raced to her uncle's office. Once inside she asked him for the keys to a vehicle and, without a word of explanation, hurried outside.

As she turned the key in the ignition, she wondered what in the world she would say when she reached Thad's apartment. She didn't have a clue. She had no plan, no program, no map to guide her through this maze. All she knew was that she had to try to plead her case. And if she failed, she'd have the rest of her life to regret it.

"I'm hungry, Daddy."

Brittany's words pulled Thad back from the edge of darkness. "What do you feel like eating, honey?" The thought of food actually repulsed him.

She studied the neon signs flying past the car window. "I like their chicken strips." She pointed to a flashing sign up ahead. "And their dipping sauce."

As he drove to the speaker and placed an order it occurred to him that his daughter was only four years old, and she knew the menu of every fast-food place in town. It was one more layer of guilt to wallow in. And he was already practically drowning in it.

By the time they got back to their apartment, he was battling a raging headache. Once inside he began assembling food on a plate while Brittany climbed up to the table.

"Heather likes their dipping sauce, too. But she says her recipe is better."

"That's nice." He filled a plastic cup with juice and sat down across from her. "I thought she didn't like to cook."

"She said she's a good cook. But she doesn't get the chance to do it often. Don't you remember?"

When he didn't answer Brittany glanced at him. "Aren't you eating, Daddy?"

"No. I'm not hungry tonight."

"Heather likes to eat."

"Yeah. I've noticed."

"I like being with Heather. She makes everything fun." The little girl paused to wipe her mouth. "Why couldn't she come home with us, Daddy?"

"Because she doesn't live here. She lives at the Colton ranch."

"But she said that isn't her real home. Have you ever seen Heather's real home, Daddy?"

"No, honey." He sighed. With every mention of that name, the knife was driven deeper. "Eat your dinner before it gets cold."

At a knock on the door he was almost relieved to escape. "You stay here and I'll see who it is."

He peered through the peephole and visibly paled. The last thing he'd wanted was another blow to the heart. But apparently that was what he was about to face.

He tore open the door and forced himself to meet those stormy blue eyes. "Heather."

Seeing the way he barred her entrance, she said simply, "May I come in?"

"Sure." He stepped aside and saw her glance around as she entered.

"Where's Brittany?"

"In the kitchen. Did you have a reason for coming here? Something you left behind?"

His words were obviously meant to cut. But she'd had plenty of time to think on her way here. She'd already steeled herself to overlook his words and try to hear the meaning beneath them.

She stepped away from the door and stood very tall, needing to hold herself together. "I'm not Vanessa, Thad."

He blinked. That wasn't at all what he'd expected to hear. "I don't know what you—"

She held up a hand to silence him. "I know you don't like to talk about her. Or about your marriage. But you told me enough to let me fill in the blanks. I'm sorry that the two of you were so badly mismatched, but that has nothing to do with you and me."

"Doesn't it?" His eyes narrowed. "Do you know how many people go from relationship to relationship, always ending up with the same situation time after time?"

"Don't quote statistics, Thad. This is about us. Or rather, about me. You've decided that because I'm young and blond and come from money, I'm a clone of your first wife. But I'm not. Look at me, Thad. I'm the same woman you couldn't wait to love."

He winced. "And as I told you, it happened before."

"But it doesn't have to happen again. You're a different man now than the one who married Vanessa. For one thing you're a father now, Thad, and that has given you a whole new perspective on life." Her voice lowered. "I know you've been hurt, and that makes you want to guard your heart. But I'd never trample on it, Thad."

"You may not want to, but you won't be able to help yourself." When she opened her mouth to protest he said, "Listen to me." He was careful not to touch her. If he did, he'd be lost. Even now, knowing he had to send her away, he wanted her. Ached for her. "I'm a cop, making do on a cop's salary. How long do you think you could go on living in this cramped apartment before you went to Daddy and asked him to buy you a big house like the one you grew up in?"

"You can't be serious. Do you really think so little of me, Thad?"

He hated the pain in her eyes. But this was for her own good. If he could just hold out a few minutes longer, he'd be doing her the biggest favor of her life. "I once told you that you can't help being who you are, any more than I can help being who I am. And what you are is the product of wealth and privilege. How could any man ask a princess to live in a hovel?"

"If he loved her enough, he'd ask. And if she loved him enough, she'd be honored to accept."

She waited, giving him one more chance to say the word that would keep her here. When he remained silent she took a step back, until she felt the door behind her.

Turning, she flung it open and paused on the threshold. "If you'd have asked me, Thad, I'd have stayed for a lifetime." She swallowed hard. "When you opened the door just now you asked if I'd left something behind. I did. It was my heart. I gave it to you, Thad. You and Brittany, trusting that you'd cherish it the way I cherish the two of you."

She ran to the car, praying she could hold back the tears.

Thad turned to see his little daughter standing in the kitchen doorway. Her eyes were wide and unblinking.

"Why did Heather look so sad, Daddy?"

He shoved his hands in his pockets and decided it was time for a little honesty. "Because I sent her away."

"Why?"

"Because I thought it was best."

"Best for who, Daddy?"

"For Heather." He walked closer and knelt down so that he was eye-level with his daughter. "Heather is young and beautiful. We have no right to ask her to spend her life with us."

"Oh." She stared into his eyes with the directness so typical of a child. "Are we going to marry someone old and ugly, Daddy?"

The question caught him so off-guard, he was rocked back on his heels. When he found his voice he muttered, "Out of the mouths of babes." He considered for several moments before saying, "Maybe, in the back of my mind, I was thinking just that. Because it would be safer somehow."

"What about in the front of your mind, Daddy?"

He nearly smiled. "In the front of my mind I think about Heather. A lot." He cleared his throat. "Do you think Heather could love us, Brittany?"

She nodded. "Uh-huh. And you know what, Daddy?"

"What, honey?"

"I think you love Heather as much as I do."

He arched a brow. "Why do you think that?"

"'Cause you look so sad." She touched a fingertip to the furrow between his brows, just the way she'd seen Heather do. "And that's the same way Heather looked when she left. And you know what else, Daddy?"

"What, honey?"

"When Heather was here with us, we were so happy. I felt like I had a real mommy."

He held her a little away and stared into her eyes, before shaking his head in wonder. "How did you get so smart?" Then he drew her close to his heart and pressed his lips to her temple. "You're right. And so was Heather. I've made a terrible mistake." He lifted her in his arms and snatched up his keys. "Come on."

"Where are we going, Daddy?"

"To make things right."

Thad tried to ignore his daughter's delighted chatter as he drove toward the Colton ranch. What could he possibly say to Heather? The truth, of course. But didn't women want more? Didn't they want the words all wrapped up in pretty paper and tied with ribbon? He was no good at this. Never had been. He was a plainspoken man. Still, he decided to rehearse a few lines. He'd tell her he'd been wrong to think she was anything like Vanessa, but he'd been trying to shield her from his own shortcomings. After all, he was no prize package.

He turned up the drive leading to the ranch and mentally cursed himself. All of that may be true, but there were different degrees of the truth. And in simple language, he'd been protecting his own heart. That was what all of this had been about. He'd been

afraid to love someone as special as Heather Mc-
Grath. Afraid that she couldn't possibly love him as
much as he loved her.

There. He'd admitted it to himself. Now if only
he could do the same to her.

He turned off the ignition and stared at the house
a moment before getting out and taking his daughter
by the hand.

They were met at the door by Inez who led them
to Joe's office. Thad glanced around, expecting to
see Heather. Instead, Joe was alone.

Joe looked up with a smile. "Hey, Thad. Hello,
Brittany."

"Hi, Joe. I'm here…we're here," he corrected,
"to see Heather."

Joe looked from Thad to his daughter and could
see the same serious expression in both pair of eyes.
"Sorry. She's gone."

"Gone where?"

"Back to San Diego. She didn't even pack, just
asked if she could take one of the cars. I told her
the new red Corvette was hers to keep. I bought it
as a gift to thank her for all the work she'd done
here."

"She's…gone for good?"

"Yeah." Joe saw a bleak look come into the detective's eyes and knew that what he'd suspected
was true. Heather and Thad must have had some sort

of lover's spat. He'd seen that same bleak look in Heather's eyes when she'd returned from town.

Joe glanced at his watch. "She's got a head start. Been gone about ten minutes now. But I suppose a smart cop would know a couple of slick ways to catch her." He paused a beat. "That is, if he really wanted to."

Thad nodded and snatched up his daughter. "Come on, Brittany. We've got to run."

Joe put a hand on his arm. "Why don't you leave Brittany here with me? I just happen to have some bubbles left." He held up a bottle and heard the little girl's squeal of delight. "And I'd think you could take a lot more risks if you're alone, Thad."

Thad turned to his daughter. "What do you say, Brittany? Want to go with me, or stay with Uncle Joe?"

"I'll stay with Uncle Joe, Daddy. As long as you promise to bring Heather back home to us."

"I promise, honey." He shot Joe a grateful look. "Thanks, my friend. I owe you."

Heather barely glanced at the passing scenery as she roared along the highway. What a difference a few weeks had made in her life. She'd arrived here with such high hopes and now she was leaving with a heart so battered and bruised, she wasn't certain it would ever heal.

She ought to hate Thad Law for what he'd done to her. But she couldn't. All she could do was hate the past that had made him so afraid to trust. Maybe some day he'd be able to move beyond this and find someone with whom he'd take a chance.

That thought cut her to the quick and she blinked hard before fiddling with the dials of the car radio. At the first blast of rock music she winced and turned it off.

In the sudden silence she thought she heard the sound of a siren. Since it seemed to be growing louder, she glanced in the rearview mirror to see a police car bearing down on her, lights flashing. She was so startled she looked around to see who it could possibly be following, but hers was the only car on this stretch of highway. Puzzled, she pulled over, and the squad car pulled up directly behind her.

A young officer strode toward her and said firmly, "Please step out of the car, ma'am."

"Step out? Why? What have I done? I wasn't speeding, Officer."

"I know that, ma'am. But I was given a description of your car and asked to hold you until backup arrived."

"Backup?" She was clearly annoyed as she opened the door of the Corvette and stepped out, trying to see beyond the mirrored glasses of the young officer.

But he gave away nothing as he stepped back a pace and glanced toward an approaching car. "Here's my backup now," he muttered as Thad slammed the car door and stalked toward them.

Thad's voice was rough with impatience. "Good work, Scott. Thanks."

"No problem, sir. I figured this must be a pretty important case."

"Yeah, Scott. The biggest of my life."

"You want me to stay and give you a hand, sir?"

"No, thanks. I can take it from here."

With a last glance at Heather, the young officer returned to his police car and drove away.

With hands on her hips Heather faced Thad. "How dare you embarrass me this—"

"Call it the desperate actions of a crazy man."

"Having me stopped by a—"

"I know. I'm sorry I had to resort to bending all the rules." He saw her look of astonishment. "Yeah. Go figure. Your Mr. Straight Arrow has been thoroughly corrupted. I've broken the cardinal rule of the force. Never allow your personal life to interfere with your professional behavior as an officer of the law. But, as I said, I'm desperate. I couldn't let you leave."

Whatever she'd been about to say died on her lips. She stopped, then tried again. "Why not?"

"Because I was wrong. About everything. And you were right. I was afraid. Afraid of taking off my blinders and seeing the truth."

"What is the truth, Thad?"

He said it simply. It was the only way he knew. "Heather, I love you. Brittany loves you. And, though we certainly don't deserve it, you love us."

She felt tears sting and blinked them back. "How can you say that? I'm still the same person I was an hour ago. Rich, spoiled. And you were right. Just look at this gift from my uncle. It's certainly more than I ever expected, but then, as you pointed out, I've been treated like a princess my whole life."

His voice was rough with feeling. "Joe told me about the Corvette. I guess I'll just have to get used to having royalty around. And if your family insists on giving you lavish gifts, I'll just have to get used to that, too." He was still afraid to touch her. Afraid that the pain he'd inflicted was too deep, her feelings too raw. "I said some terrible things. Can you find it in your heart to forgive me?"

She stared deeply into his eyes, trying to read his thoughts. The pain and remorse were there. As deeply felt, she thought, as her own feelings. "I might be persuaded."

"I'll do anything, Heather. Anything to make it right between us."

She felt the beginnings of a smile touch the corners of her lips. "Anything?"

He nodded. "Name it. If it's within my power, I'll get it for you. Just say I'm forgiven."

She waited a minute longer, willing her heartbeat to slow down. Then she touched a hand to his arm. "I can't stay angry with you, Thad."

He closed his eyes for a moment, too overcome to speak. When he opened them he got down on his knees in the dirt. "I don't want a weekend lover, Heather. I want a wife. I'm talking about marriage. About forever. If you'll have me."

For one brief moment Heather felt her heart actually leap before it began a wild dance. She looked into those deep blue eyes and wondered how she could have ever thought them cold. There was such fire in them now. A blaze that started a similar fire in her heart.

She caught his hands and brought him to his feet. "It's what I want, too, Thad. Forever."

"You'll marry me?"

"I will."

He stared at their joined hands, then dragged her close and kissed her, long and slow and deep, and felt the blaze become an inferno.

When at last he lifted his head he was smiling.

That quick, dangerous smile she'd come to love. "Brittany is going to be so happy. She already thinks of us as a family."

"Family." Heather touched a hand to her heart. "You have no idea how much I love the sound of that word. Where is Brittany?"

"With your Uncle Joe."

She caught his hand. "Come on. Let's go tell her the news."

He held back and drew her firmly into his arms, covering her mouth with his in a kiss so hot, so hungry, it had them both trembling.

Against her mouth he whispered, "We'll tell her. In a little while. But first, I need to just hold you." And then, as he took the kiss deeper he muttered, "I wonder if there's a law against a police detective making love with his woman in a brand-new Corvette?"

His woman. She loved the sound of that.

"Admit it, Detective." She gave him a sultry smile. "It's not really such a hardship loving a rich woman, is it?"

"I suppose it might have its compensations."

"Speaking of which, I believe you owe me five dollars. That bet, remember? You thought I couldn't last in Prosperino for two weeks. And now we're talking about forever."

"You see? More corruption of a police officer. What am I going to do about you?"

They both laughed.

"I guess you're just going to have to resign yourself to the fact that you're in love with a wild, wicked woman."

"Wild, maybe. But never wicked." As his laughter faded, he pressed her back against the car and kissed her.

A car roared past, the driver honking and shouting something unintelligible as he sped away.

"Thad." Heather pressed a hand to his chest, knowing how he valued his reputation. "We're in a very public place. Somebody might recognize you."

He kissed her again, hard and quick, and muttered against her lips, "I've wasted too much time worrying about the wrong things. Right now, nothing matters except being with you. I was so afraid I'd driven you away. And now that you're here in my arms, I'm never letting you go."

She gave a sigh that came straight from her heart. "I do love you, Thad. I truly believe that we're destined to stay together for a lifetime."

"A lifetime." The word was a moan of pleasure as he added, "I won't settle for anything less. I want you with me for eternity."

And then there was no need for words as they told each other, in the way that lovers have from the beginning of time, all the feelings that had been locked away in their hearts.

*The Colton family saga
continues next month with Laurie Paige's
THE HOUSEKEEPER'S DAUGHTER,
December 2001. Don't miss it!*

One

Maya Ramirez breathed deeply of the crystalline air and let it out in a long exhalation. The accompanying sigh was not exactly one of contentment—too many disturbing things had happened on the Colton ranch the past eight months for contentment to prevail—but at least she had found a certain peace of mind concerning her own future.

Her horse, a sweet mare named Penny for the coppery highlights of her coat, twitched one ear in her direction. Maya patted the mare's neck and admired the scenery.

It was one of those February days along the coast

of northern California in which the sky gleamed a breath-catching blue and the temperature had soared into the sixties after a week of cold, drizzly rain. Today, the cloud bank had receded offshore and all was bright and beautiful. For the first time in months, anything seemed possible.

Almost anything, Maya corrected, batting away a lazy bee that hummed over the lupine that was already beginning to flower in stalks of white, yellow and lavender blue.

"A hawk," ten-year-old Joe Colton, Jr., yelled, pointing at the long, sweeping line of fifty-foot cliffs that scalloped the ocean along the western border of the ranch.

"Where?" Teddy Colton, younger by two years, called.

"Right there, silly— Uh, right there," Joe amended with a quick glance at Maya.

She gave him an approving nod, then smiled with affection. She didn't allow name-calling or insults. Although newly employed as their full-time nanny, she'd been baby-sitting the boys for years, being only sixteen when she'd first been asked to accompany Mrs. Colton to a spa and take care of Joe, Jr., who had been a baby at the time.

Ten years ago. Maya sighed and shifted in the saddle, the sudden sting of tears surprising her as she contemplated the passage of time—so fast and yet so slow.

When Mrs. Colton had had Teddy, Maya had helped out with him, too. After graduating from the local high school, she'd started college via computer courses and worked on the Colton estate when needed by her mother, who was the housekeeper there.

Last month she'd been asked to move into the main house and take over as a full-time baby-sitter for the two youngest Colton boys. The nanny, Ms. Meredith called her. Frowning, Maya admitted she'd needed the job rather desperately.

She swatted another bee out of her face, then noticed several others crawling in Penny's mane. The mare shook her head as one landed on her ear. Maya realized the warm weather had caused a swarm.

"Can we race?" Teddy shouted, giving her an appealing glance from his blue eyes.

She nodded. "I think we're running into a swarm of bees. Turn back toward the ranch and ease into a canter. Don't swat the bees. They'll fly off if you leave them alone and don't scare them."

Both boys glanced around anxiously, but they kept their heads and did as told. After making sure they were on their way, she turned the mare, who switched her tail to each side and shook her head again. Gently Maya urged the mare into a fast walk, then past a trot into a loping run.

In front of her, the brothers let out a whoop of excitement and raced toward the stable in the distance. She leaned forward with a grimace and tightened her knees, but she couldn't keep up the pace. After reining the mare back to a fast walk, she relaxed once more.

The mare repeatedly shook her head as they neared the paddock. Her ears twitched nervously.

Maya patted her on the neck. "Hey, pretty Penny, what's the matter, girl? The bees are gone—"

She got no further when the horse gave a startled whinny, tossed her head and, without warning, took off at a dead run toward the stable. Maya grabbed the saddle horn and held on for dear life, fear rushing over her as she thought of falling.

The adrenaline boost gave her the strength to rise in the stirrups so that her weight shifted to her legs and her thighs acted as shock absorbers during the wild ride across the pasture. She pulled on the reins, but the mare raced on, heedless of the rider's commands.

Ahead of her, she saw the boys dismount and stare at her in confusion. Then a man leaped on the horse Joe had been riding and raced toward her.

Maya saw the fence looming fifty yards in front of her and knew she would never make the jump.

Neither would the mare with the extra weight of a rider and saddle on her back. "Whoa," she called desperately and pulled on the reins to turn the frightened horse to the side.

Hearing hoofbeats coming up behind her, she glanced over her shoulder. The other rider was circling toward them. He closed in and raced alongside her.

"Kick free and come to me," he yelled.

She slid her feet out of the stirrups and leaped into his arms just as he reached for her. He turned his mount and they ran alongside the fence. Penny fell in behind them and followed. Gradually he slowed his horse, then stopped.

In the stillness, there was only the sound of the two horses and the two humans, panting from the wild exertion of the run. His arms enclosed her in a blanket of safety.

It was like coming home.

"What the hell were you thinking, riding like that in your condition?" Drake Colton demanded, his golden-brown eyes flashing like molten rock in the afternoon sun, his gaze hot with fury.

So much for illusions. "I think my horse got a bee in her ear," Maya said defensively, fighting a ridiculous urge to burst into tears now that the danger was over.

She was pressed to his chest in a vise grip. His

heart pounded against hers, which was also beating hard with the aftermath of the fear when her horse bolted and with a new fear as his eyes raked down her figure.

She struggled to push away from his heat and his anger, the vibrant masculinity that called to something equally vibrant inside her. "I can walk," she told him, forcing herself to ignore the unruly needs that clamored for attention inside her.

Memories of lying snug in his arms for hours and hours overcame common sense—the warmth of his embrace, the way his hands moved on her, his sudden smile. She closed her eyes and foolishly wished for things that were never going to happen. But a person could dream....

Drake returned to the stable. There, he let her gently slide to the ground, then dropped down beside her. "Here, boys, take care of the horses."

Drake's two youngest brothers, big-eyed with worry, took the reins, then stood there and looked from their older brother to their nanny as if afraid to leave them alone.

"I'm not going to hurt her," Drake assured them in harsh tones, then added for her ears alone, "yet."

"Ask River to check Penny's ear. I think she was stung by one of the bees," Maya called to the youngsters, ignoring the threat from the furious man beside her as the fears and dreams, the need to cry, faded into fatalistic calm.

She had thought this moment might come someday. But not so soon. She wasn't ready, hadn't prepared...

After the boys led the horses off to the stable, Drake turned back to Maya. It hurt to look at her, at the thick, dark splendor of her hair, the endless depths of her brown eyes and most of all, at the protruding mound of her tummy.

"Just how pregnant are you, anyway?" he demanded, which wasn't at all what he'd planned to say to her upon his arrival at the ranch thirty minutes ago. At that time, he'd planned a calm, reasonable approach to their problems.

"What do you care?" she asked, so softly he almost didn't hear. Then she walked away without a backward glance, leaving him standing in the dust, his heart pounding with emotions he couldn't describe.

THE COLTONS

Silhouette®
Where love comes alive™

If you've enjoyed getting to know **THE COLTONS**,
Silhouette® invites you to come back and
visit the Colton family!

Just collect three (3) proofs of
purchase from the backs of three (3) different
COLTONS titles and receive a free **COLTONS**
book that's not currently available in retail outlets!

Just complete the order form and send it, along with three
(3) proofs of purchase from three (3) different **COLTONS**
titles, to: **THE COLTONS**, P.O. Box 9047, Buffalo, NY
14269-9047, or P.O. Box 613, Fort Erie, Ontario L2A 5X3.

(No cost for shipping and handling.)

- -

Name: _____

Address: _____ City: _____

State/Prov.: _____ Zip/Postal Code: _____

Please specify which title(s) you would like to receive:

❏ 0-373-38716-4 *PROTECTING PEGGY* by Maggie Price
❏ 0-373-38717-2 *SWEET CHILD OF MINE* by Jean Brashear
❏ 0-373-38718-0 *CLOSE PROXIMITY* by Donna Clayton
❏ 0-373-38719-9 *A HASTY WEDDING* by Cara Colter

Remember—for each title selected, you must send three (3)
original proofs of purchase. To receive *all four (4)* titles, just send
in all twelve (12) proofs of purchase.

(Please allow 4-6 weeks for delivery.
Offer good while quantities last.
Offer available in Canada and the U.S. only.)
(The proof of purchase should be cut off the ad.)

THE COLTONS
ONE PROOF OF PURCHASE
COLTPOP-R2

093 KIJ DAET   Visit Silhouette at www.eHarlequin.com   COLTPOP-R2

CALL THE ONES YOU LOVE OVER THE HOLIDAYS!

Save $25 off future book purchases when you buy any four Harlequin® or Silhouette® books in October, November and December 2001,

PLUS

receive a phone card good for 15 minutes of long-distance calls to anyone you want in North America!

WHAT AN INCREDIBLE DEAL!

Just fill out this form and attach 4 proofs of purchase (cash register receipts) from October, November and December 2001 books, and Harlequin Books will send you a coupon booklet worth a total savings of $25 off future purchases of Harlequin® and Silhouette® books, AND a 15-minute phone card to call the ones you love, anywhere in North America.

Please send this form, along with your cash register receipts as proofs of purchase, to:
In the USA: Harlequin Books, P.O. Box 9057, Buffalo, NY 14269-9057
In Canada: Harlequin Books, P.O. Box 622, Fort Erie, Ontario L2A 5X3
Cash register receipts must be dated no later than December 31, 2001.
Limit of 1 coupon booklet and phone card per household.
Please allow 4-6 weeks for delivery.

> **I accept your offer! Enclosed are 4 proofs of purchase.**
> **Please send me my coupon booklet**
> **and a 15-minute phone card:**
>
> Name: _____
> Address: _____ City: _____
> State/Prov.: _____ Zip/Postal Code: _____
> Account Number (if available): _____

097 KJB DAGL
PHQ4013

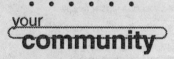

INTIMATE MOMENTS™

and NATIONAL BESTSELLING AUTHOR
RUTH LANGAN

present her brand-new miniseries

Lives—and hearts—are on the line when the Lassiters pledge to uphold the law at any cost.

Available November 2001
BY HONOR BOUND (IM #1111)

Eldest brother Micah Lassiter discovers the dangers of mixing business and pleasure when he falls for the beautiful woman he's been hired to protect.

Available January 2002
RETURN OF THE PRODIGAL SON (IM #1123)

Ex-C.I.A. agent Donovan Lassiter learns the true meaning of love when he comes to the rescue of a young widow and her two small children.

And coming in spring 2002
Mary-Brendan and Cameron Lassiter's stories

Available at your favorite retail outlet.

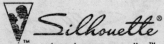

Where love comes alive™

Celebrate the season with

Midnight Clear

A holiday anthology featuring
a classic Christmas story from
New York Times bestselling author

Debbie Macomber

Plus a brand-new *Morgan's Mercenaries* story
from *USA Today* bestselling author

Lindsay McKenna

And a brand-new *Twins on the Doorstep* story
from national bestselling author

Stella Bagwell

Available at your favorite retail outlets in November 2001!

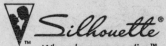

If you enjoyed what you just read,
then we've got an offer you can't resist!

Take 2
bestselling novels FREE!
Plus get a FREE surprise gift!

THE COLTONS

If you missed the first five exciting stories
from **THE COLTONS**, here's a chance
to order your copies today!

Silhouette®